HOME AGAIN

RACHEL HANNA

CHAPTER 1

*E*mmy Moore sat at the round table and held her head in her hands. This had to be rock bottom. Any lower, and she would be underground.

Even her elbows were sweating with anxiety, something she had no idea was even possible. But sure enough, they were sticky and causing the mound of legal papers and spreadsheets to adhere to her skin.

"Emmy? You haven't said anything in the last ten minutes. Are you still with me?"

She had trusted him. He was her husband after all. Now, he would soon be her ex-husband, and she would soon be an ex-business owner. Amazing what putting on blinders can do to someone's life.

Blind trust was never going to be an option for her again.

She'd met Steve in their first year of college all those years ago. He'd always been a dreamer, and he'd told her that he was an entrepreneur at heart. That although he was getting his degree in political science, he wanted to open a restaurant one day.

When Emmy's career as a physical therapist took off

several years later, Steve had talked her into investing money into his big dream. So, together they opened the restaurant two years ago. Until this moment, she had no idea the mess he'd made.

"Emmy? You're worrying me."

Emmy finally raised her head up and stared at her friend and accountant, Eloise Donavan. The older woman had done her taxes for years, and she trusted her guidance. She was one of the few people she still trusted in this crazy world.

"Can you just repeat to me… one more time… what is going on?" Emmy asked, staring at the "closed" sign on the front door of the restaurant. It was lunch time. The place should be teeming with patrons right about now.

"The bank has called your loan due, sweetie. Steve hasn't paid the mortgage on the building in months. And your vendors won't deliver anymore. He hasn't paid your meat vendor in about four months…"

"Okay, stop…. Please…" Emmy put her head back in her hands. She wondered how it was possible to have such a massive headache so early in the day.

"I'm so sorry, Emmy. I really am."

"But you were watching the books, right?"

Eloise sighed. "Not for the last three months. Steve… stopped paying me too."

"Why didn't you tell me?" Emmy asked, looking up at her friend.

"I didn't want to worry you. Steve always told me you were just the financial backer, but I was to bring all financial concerns to him. I was already planning to talk to you about it when all of these notices started showing up. Steve took the paying power away from me when it came to the mortgage. Said he'd handle that himself…"

Emmy snorted. "Yeah, he did a great job."

"Maybe you two can sit down and talk…"

"He served me with divorce papers yesterday."

Eloise's eyes grew wide. "I had no idea."

Emmy stood up and walked to the window overlooking the city streets of Atlanta. It was a cool, crisp spring day - her favorite time of year. The sunlight was bouncing off the glassy skyscrapers, and people were busy milling about on the sidewalks surrounding her small restaurant. The sight of it all used to bring her joy. But right now, she wanted to curl up into the fetal position until winter came.

"Things were good in our early years, but not so good since we opened this place. I thought if I kept my career and we didn't actually work side by side every day that this business wouldn't affect our relationship. Turns out I was wrong."

"But I don't understand. Why does Steve want a divorce? Seems like he'd need you now more than ever."

"Remember that hot little blond bartender he hired a few months back?" Emmy asked, turning back toward the table. Eloise nodded. "Turns out he needs *her* now more than he needs me."

"Yuck. Sometimes men suck," Eloise huffed.

"Well, today is one of those days," Emmy said, not even arguing with her friend that women cheat on men too. Right now, she just needed to believe that men sucked and it was okay to say it out loud. "So, what now?"

"Well, I think you need to consult with your attorney about the legal ramifications and so forth. They can help figure out what you owe and what Steve owes..."

"Can't get blood out of a turnip, and Steve is definitely a turnip."

Eloise stood up and hugged Emmy. "I'm here if you need me, okay? Any time. Day or night."

Emmy smiled half heartedly. "Thanks. I really do appreciate it."

As she watched Eloise walk out of the restaurant, she felt sick. This place had all of her savings tied up, and there was no way to get it back out again. She was a smart woman, and she knew that everything would be liquidated to pay at least some of her debts.

Her mother, before she moved into the retirement village in Whiskey Ridge, had told her that giving Steve *her* savings to pursue *his* dreams was dumb. She hadn't believed her at the time, but maybe she was right.

Just then, her cell phone rang with an unknown number. She normally ignored those, especially now that they would probably be collectors, but she decided to take a chance and answer it.

"Hello?"

"Ms. Moore?"

"Yes…" She wasn't yet used to being called her maiden name again, but she'd already decided she was changing it back. Her marriage to Steve would be over soon, and she didn't even want his last name as a reminder.

"This is Catherine at the Whiskey Ridge Retirement Village."

"Is my mother alright?" Emmy immediately asked.

"Oh, yes. She's fine. But we need to meet with you about something rather pressing. Can you come by today?"

"I live in Atlanta so it's about a two-hour drive. But I could come by tomorrow morning around ten. Would that work?"

There was a pause. "Yes. I suppose that will be okay. But please do come. It's quite important that we speak with you."

DRIVING into Whiskey Ridge was not what Emmy expected to be doing today. In actuality, she needed to get away from her current situation. The city reminded her of Steve and all of the lies she'd believed.

Like the one where he promised to be faithful and then spent their money on his secret girlfriend. Or the one where he promised to be responsible with her life savings but apparently took his girlfriend gambling for the weekend when he was supposed to be away on business securing a new meat vendor. She'd found that one out overnight during a call with her attorney. She'd also learned he wasn't a good gambler and much of even her small savings had been lost on bad business decisions and gambling trips masquerading as "business".

Who was this man? And how did she fall for someone who disrespected her and their marriage so much? Her brain was starting to hurt, so she turned her attention back to the passing scenery.

She usually only came back to her small mountain home-town if she was visiting her mother, which she hadn't done since moving her into the retirement home a few months ago. And even then, she'd crept into town quietly, stayed for the day and then jetted her way straight back to Atlanta as fast as she could.

She loved her mother, but growing up with her hadn't been easy. First of all, she had no filter between her brain and mouth. She said what she thought, even if it wasn't politically correct. Secondly, she stood out like a sore thumb among the older, Southern, genteel ladies of the small mountain town.

All of her life, Emmy had been known as "Pauline's daughter" around Whiskey Ridge. Her mother, an eccentric painter and the loudest dresser she knew, had a personality that overshadowed anyone else Emmy had ever met.

And while a great, big personality wasn't necessarily a bad thing, Pauline often took it to the extreme, wanting the attention on herself more and more as she got older. Which is why Steve had put his foot down when Emmy floated the idea of her mother moving in with them in Atlanta after she started having issues being on her own.

In all reality, Pauline never would've agreed to move to the big city anyway. She often said she'd only leave Whiskey Ridge one way and that was in a casket. Although even that didn't make sense because her burial plot was smack dab in the middle of the Whiskey Ridge Cemetery.

Whiskey Ridge certainly held a special place in Emmy's heart as it was the place she grew up, but the moment she could fly the coop, she did. There were too many memories, too much pain, to keep her there once she was an adult.

She pulled into the retirement community parking lot and just sat for a moment, staring at the blue tinged mountains behind the building. The mountains towered over the small town like a protector, yet they had sometimes made her feel stifled and sheltered as a kid. Everyone knew everyone else in their town, and gossip was served on everybody's dinner plate in the evening.

Yet, she found herself missing it all right now. The simplicity. The familiarity. The seclusion. Right now, she wanted to wrap herself up in all of it and block out the world she was currently living in that included legal documents, divorce decrees and a pile of bills that rivaled any mountain.

But she couldn't run away. Because inside of those double doors lived her mother. Her wild and crazy and untamed mother who was likely causing some sort of problem that Emmy would have to sort out. Like she'd done her whole life.

She stepped out of her compact car, the one Steve had encouraged her to buy and then apparently stopped paying for. Thankfully, she had been able to catch those payments up so at least she wouldn't be losing her only source of transportation.

Taking in a deep breath, she remembered the smell of the

mountain air. So clean and crisp in early spring, she could smell the aroma of tulips growing down near the town square.

"Good morning. Can I help you?" the young woman asked when Emmy walked to the front desk.

"Yes. I'm here to meet with Catherine about my mother... Pauline Moore."

The woman's eyebrows raised just a bit, but then she smiled as if she was sorry. "Right. Okay. Let me just tell her that you're here." She stepped away into an adjoining office and left Emmy feeling like this might be worse than she thought.

A few moments later, a conservative woman with brown hair appeared in the lobby. She had her hair swept up into a bun and looked way more corporate than Emmy was used to seeing in Whiskey Ridge.

"Ms. Moore? I'm Catherine Jacobs."

"Nice to meet you. Please, call me Emmy."

She shook Catherine's hand and followed her into the office, taking a seat in a floral upholstered chair in front of the desk. For some reason, she felt like she was on a job interview.

"Thank you for coming all the way here this morning, Emmy. I want to say first that I wouldn't have bothered you if this wasn't an urgent situation."

"Is everything okay with my mother? Is she ill?"

Catherine looked down at her papers and then met Emmy's eyes. "Your mother has to move out of our community, Emmy."

Emmy stared at Catherine like she had two heads. Her mother was being kicked out of a retirement home? Was that even possible?

"Excuse me?"

"Your mother has been... how do I put this... a bit of a

problem here. We can no longer allow her to be a disruption to the other residents and staff."

"With all due respect, what on Earth could an elderly woman possibly do to get expelled from a retirement home?"

Catherine pulled a paper out of her file and began reading a long list of offenses from it.

"Flooded the hallway bathroom trying to make water balloons after stealing them from the party supply room... Stole Gertrude's false teeth and put them in a plastic Halloween pumpkin she found in another closet... Prank called local residents from the phone in the office... Called 911 hoping, as she put it, 'hot' firefighters would come... Attempted to sneak out and hot wire the van so she could go on an adventure to the local beauty supply store..."

"Stop!" Emmy said, putting her hand up and closing her eyes. She took a deep breath. "Okay, look, I'll admit that my mother is a bit... quirky. She always has been. She likes to have a good time..."

"Emmy, these things are just the tip of the ice berg. Your mother requires constant supervision, almost like a toddler. We've had to pay for more staff just to make sure she doesn't hurt anyone, including herself. I'm sorry, but you're going to need to take your mother home today."

"Wait. What? Today?"

"Yes. We've already boxed her things. She doesn't know yet, though, so..."

"Oh I get it. So I have to tell her too?" Emmy asked, standing up. Could her life go any more off the rails?

"Please try to see this from our perspective."

"I can't do this. I live in Atlanta. She'll never go to the city, and I can't come back here. I have a career and a home... There's got to be something we can work out. What about another facility?"

"We already checked into that. She's not ill enough for a

nursing home or even assisted living. But no retirement home is going to take her after her... record."

"She has a permanent record? Really?" Emmy couldn't believe what she was hearing. She almost wanted to laugh, but it would've been one of those crazy, deranged laughs that may have scared poor Catherine even more.

"I hate to cut this short, but I really need to get back to the residents. Today is our spring musical practice." Catherine plastered a fake smile on her face and waited for Emmy to stand.

Emmy sighed. She would have no choice but to pick up her mother and move her back to her house a few streets over, which thankfully hadn't sold yet. Whiskey Ridge's real estate market wasn't exactly fast paced.

Catherine led her through the maze of hallways to the TV room where her mother was sitting watching some judge show. While the other women around her were knitting or quietly chatting, Pauline was shouting at the TV with her thoughts on some case about an unpaid car repair.

"Throw the book at him!" she yelled, pumping her fist in the air.

"Mother," Emmy said from behind. Pauline turned and her eyes went wide when she saw her daughter standing there.

"Emmy? Well, I'll be a hot potato! What in the world are you doing here?" She stood up, and Emmy got quite a show with her mother's outfit - a pair of hot pink capri pants and a bulky black sweatshirt bedazzled with neon green sequins. Not to mention her leopard print fuzzy slippers that she had begged for two Christmases ago.

Pauline hugged her daughter tightly, although Emmy wasn't really in the mood to reciprocate. Right now, she wanted to wring her mother's neck for adding to her already overwhelming stress levels.

"I'll just give you two a moment to talk," Catherine said softly before walking away.

"You know, Cathy, you need to let your hair down if you wanna catch a man!" Pauline called back with a loud laugh. The other older women in the room cut their eyes at her, a fact that did not go unnoticed to Emmy. This was just one of the many embarrassing moments her mother had created in her life.

"Mom! Stop it!" Emmy whispered loudly. "Let's go out into the courtyard and have a talk."

"Oh good Lord..." Pauline said as she followed her daughter to the door leading to the small courtyard.

When they got outside, Emmy sat down on one of the concrete benches while Pauline sat in a rocking chair next to the koi pond. She pulled some spare croutons out of her pocket - why she had them there, Emmy hadn't a clue - and tossed them to the waiting orange fish.

She looked at her mother for a moment before speaking. The whole reason Pauline had agreed to move to the retirement home was because she was starting to forget things. She would forget where her keys were. What time church started. That she had put a sweet potato in the wall oven. One day, Emmy had come for a long overdue visit to find her mother's kitchen filled with a sweet smelling smoke and found the charred sweet potato still cooking while her mother watched Wheel of Fortune.

And then there was the car accident where her mother "forgot" to stop at the stop sign and rammed another car. Thankfully, the other driver was fine, but Pauline had hurt her knee and needed rehab.

It soon became apparent to Emmy that her mother needed someone to watch over her, and given her big personality... well, that was hard to find in their small town.

Most people liked Pauline. She entertained them. But no

one wanted to get too close for too long because she was too unpredictable. So when the retirement community opened up last fall - and brought with it outside employees who didn't know Pauline - it seemed like the perfect fit.

Until it wasn't.

"Mom, I don't know how to say this…"

"These stiffs want me to move out. Right?" she asked, looking at her daughter with that determined glare only Pauline Moore could give.

"Yes."

"Good. I'm ready to get back to my house." Pauline looked down at the fish and tossed the last of her crumbled up croutons. "Bye, fishies!"

"You can't just go home, Mom."

"And why the hell not? I'm a grown woman."

"Because you know you were forgetful. And then the car accident…"

"I don't have Alzheimer's!" Pauline would get very defensive about the thought she might have the disease that would steal her memory and eventually her life. So far, doctors just weren't sure if she was in the beginning stages or it was just a product of aging, so Pauline preferred to think it was just some kind of passing phase that late 60-somethings get.

"I never said you did. But the fact remains that I can't leave you in Whiskey Ridge at your house alone. We're going to have to find full-time care or something…"

"No. I don't want some stranger in my house with me all the time. They might steal my stuff!"

Emmy had to struggle not to laugh at that one. Her mother didn't have valuables. She had "collections", and no one wanted them. Collections of doll heads. Collections of tacky handbags. Collections of half-done paintings that were quirky to say the least.

"Mom, you have to work with me here. I can't stay in Whiskey Ridge. I have a life back in Atlanta."

"Sure you do."

Emmy sighed. "And just what is that supposed to mean?"

"You know, I might be getting a little long in the tooth, but I'm no fool, Emmy Lou."

Gosh, how she hated her middle name.

"What are you getting at?"

"I know something's going on with you and Steve."

"And how do you know that?"

"Because mothers know these things. I just have a feeling."

"Well, you're wrong," Emmy said, trying to hide her face because it always gave her away.

"Don't lie to me, child," Pauline said sternly as she eyed her daughter. Emmy froze in place and then slouched into her seat further.

"Okay. Fine. We're getting a divorce, Mom. Happy now?"

Pauline stood and came to sit beside her daughter. "I'm not happy you're going through that, but I am happy that you're getting rid of that bum. He never deserved you, Em. And now you can find someone who is worthy."

Emmy laughed. "Yeah, I'm not interested in finding another man anytime soon. Trust me."

Pauline took her daughter's hand. "I want to go home. I know I can be a bit of a pain sometimes, but why don't you stay with me for awhile? It'll help both of us."

"I can't." Even as she said it, she knew the choices were few. But the thought of coming home to Whiskey Ridge and dealing with her mother's craziness was almost too much to bear.

"You mean you won't."

"Mom, I have a career in Atlanta. I have a home there, and the restaurant." No need to tell her about the mess she was really in back in the city.

Pauline looked at Emmy, and it was one of those rare times she was serious. "Did you know that we get moments in our lives where all of the wrongs can be made right? Not everybody gets that chance, but when you do... well, you should take it."

Emmy wasn't totally sure what that meant, but she knew that the option of going back to Whiskey Ridge suddenly felt less scary than the option of going home and having her problems smack her in the face on a daily basis.

CHAPTER 2

"*Y*ou know you're freaking lucky to be alive, right?"
Nash Collier stared out the window of his hospital room overlooking the Las Vegas skyline. He would much rather be playing the slots right now than sitting in a hospital room with his leg hiked up in the air and his arm in a sling.

"I've fallen off a bull a million times, Deke," he said to one of his rodeo buddies - actually one of his fellow competitors. He and Deke had traveled the country together for almost ten years now, so he was more like a brother than someone he competed with.

"Man, I get it. But we're not getting any younger, and those bulls ain't getting any smaller or slower. Maybe it's time to..."

"Shut it." Nash didn't like to hear talk about packing it in and settling down. The rodeo was in his blood and always had been. From his earliest days back in Whiskey Ridge, Georgia, his father had instilled a work ethic in him that never died.

As the owner of the South's second largest rodeo events

company, Nash's father had pushed him to succeed. Be the best. Break out of Whiskey Ridge and compete with the big boys. And he had done that for years, winning title after title.

He'd been the best in the South, and then the largest rodeo outfit out West had "drafted" him, so to speak. Nash's father - aptly nicknamed Brick because of his towering build - had stopped speaking to him the day he called to say he was signing a contract with another company. It had been years since they'd spoken, and Nash had soldiered on continuing to win titles. Continuing to be the best. Continuing to avoid his father and the memories lurking around every corner of his hometown.

Until last night.

The crappy part had been that he didn't go down in battle. No, he went down in practice when he fell the wrong way and then a bull stepped on him. Deke was right - he could have died. Guys had died that way before him. One inch either way, and he'd likely be paralyzed at the very least.

He had numerous injuries, some of which even he didn't understand. The doctor had rattled off a lot this morning, but all Nash heard was "out of commission for at least a few months" and "may be the end of his career".

No way was he letting that happen.

"Mr. Collier. Glad to see you're awake and alert this morning. You had us pretty nervous last night," the doctor said as he entered the room with a tablet in his hand.

"Always good to hear the doc was nervous," Nash mumbled under his breath. "When can I get out of here?"

"Where do you plan to go?" the doctor asked with a chuckle.

"Back to my house," Nash said, referring to the house he'd been renting in Vegas for the last couple of years. Since most of his competitions were out West now, he'd finally relocated a few years ago.

Deke looked at the doctor and then rolled his eyes. "Dude, you can't just go home. Doc says it's going to be months of intensive rehab. We might be roomies, but you know I have to travel..."

Hearing Deke say those words - that he'd be traveling on while Nash was laid up like some crippled has been - tore his guts out. He wanted to be on the road. It was who he was. Without rodeo, he had no idea who he was. It calmed him. Made him focus. Kept the memories at bay.

"Have you called your father yet, Mr. Collier?" the doctor asked hesitantly.

Nash stared at him and his jaw tightened.

"No."

"Don't you think you need to?" Deke interjected. "It's the only option, man. You need help, and out here you'll be alone."

Nash gave the doctor a look that let him know he needed to be alone with his friend. When the doctor had exited the room and shut the door behind him, he turned his attention back to Deke.

"I'm a grown man, and I'll do what I want. Understand?"

Deke sat down at the end of his bed, being careful not to bump his leg. "Stop being a stubborn jackass, Nash. You and I both know you have to go home. At least for a little while. Take some time. Reassess..."

"Stop preaching at me," Nash said, leaning back and sighing.

"I'll call the airlines," Deke said as he stood back up. Nash didn't make eye contact, a sure sign that he was agreeing with his friend but too proud to admit it. "You know, if you'd get a woman then she could take care of you." His attempt at a joke fell flat as Nash continued being quiet until he left the room.

~

"THIS PLACE STINKS LIKE A WHOREHOUSE!" Pauline shouted as they crossed the threshold into her home. The place had been closed up tight for months now, with not even a nibble in the slow Whiskey Ridge real estate market.

"Mama, honestly. Can you filter that mouth of yours even a little bit?" Emmy walked around the living room, lifting the plastic mini blinds and then swatting the mounds of dust that flew out each time she pulled on one of the yellowed strings.

"Why? Nobody can hear me," Pauline replied as she plopped down in her favorite, albeit ugly, chair. It was an antique and had been beautiful once. But then Pauline had seen fit to have it re-covered in the most God-awful orange and green fabric with these little dancing bears on it. Emmy had no idea where she'd found it, but she planned to get it reupholstered one day. "Why does it smell so bad in here?"

Emmy looked around and then noticed an empty bottle of Pauline's tacky perfume lying on the floor. It had seeped into the carpet and probably even into the original hardwood floors underneath it.

"This maybe?" Emmy said, holding up the frosted pink bottle and pinching her nose with her other hand. Without a word, she opened the back door and tossed it into the woods behind the house.

"Hey! That was a nice bottle. I can reuse that..." Pauline started to say as she stood up.

"No. Absolutely not. You are not bringing that back into this house. As it stands, I need to call a cleaning crew out here. And this carpet needs to be removed. It's old and dingy anyway. We'll have Abe Kramer come out with his boys and refinish these hardwood floors. That should get rid of this smell..."

"Jeez, can you calm down a little bit?" her mother said, sighing and leaning her head back against the chair. "You've always been too uptight, Em. If we're going to live together, you've got to loosen up."

"We're not 'living together', Mother," Emmy said, using air quotes. "We're not roomies. I'm simply staying here with you until we figure out a long term solution to this problem." She walked into the kitchen and looked around, wondering what she could do to spruce the place up so that it was livable to her. Right now, she felt like she'd landed back in the 70s.

"And just what problem are we trying to solve?" Pauline asked, standing in the doorway of the kitchen with her hand on her hip.

Emmy drew in a deep breath and turned around. "Mom, you know what problem we have. I have a life, and you can't stay here alone. And I can't... won't... move back to Whiskey Ridge permanently. You're going to need... care."

"Care? And just what in blue blazes does that mean? I'm not some elderly person, Emmy. I just... forget... sometimes. We all do that!" With that, Pauline stomped down the short hallway to her bedroom and slammed the door.

~

NASH STOOD at the edge of the towering deck attached to the back of his father's sprawling log cabin on the outskirts of Whiskey Ridge. This was the place he'd once called home. The place where he'd had Christmases and played fetch with his dog and shot his BB gun at cans perched precariously on the tree stump out back.

But this wasn't home anymore. Growing from a boy to a man hadn't come without consequences, the main one being that he wasn't what his father wanted him to be. He'd wanted him to help run the family business, make his money for the good of the family and not just himself.

But Nash longed to get away from his roots. From memories better forgotten. From painful reminders of things he'd lost. And a raging bull seemed to be the best answer to all of those problems.

Bulls didn't care about your feelings. They didn't care about your past or your future. They cared about getting you the hell off their back, and Nash felt much the same way. His history was like a boulder weighing him down, pushing him lower and lower, and ironically the bulls were the only things that got him back up again when he needed it. Until one stepped on him, of course.

Coming home to his father hadn't been easy. Deke had helped as much as he could with a quick trip to bring him back to Georgia before he took off for the next championship.

There would be no more championships in Nash's future unless a miracle happened. If injuries didn't get him, getting older would. His body was already breaking down in ways that men his age didn't experience. It was only a matter of time before he would have to make some tough life decisions, but not in one of his innermost thoughts did he ever see himself in Whiskey Ridge again.

It wasn't like the town wasn't a beautiful place to grow up, with its expansive blue tinged mountains, its crystal clear streams and its friendly people.

But then there were also the gossips and the constant reminders of mistakes made, love lost and disappointment. Most of the disappointment was housed in his father's eyes when he looked at him. At least that's how he perceived it anyway.

So far, his father had tiptoed around any arguments with his son, but Nash could feel it boiling beneath the surface. He knew Brick wanted to say things to him, comments he'd probably held in for years. He knew he didn't want to be the caretaker of the son who'd basically abandoned him years ago. But he had a poker face, and right now he was using it big time.

"So Deke tells me Avery Blinn won the title with that bull we saw out in El Paso that time? I figured that damn thing was dead long ago," his father said, trying to make small talk from the log hewn chair at the corner of the deck.

It was a cool day. Nash wasn't used to the weather in Whiskey Ridge anymore. Nevada tended to be hot and dry.

"Yeah. Thought so too." He often found himself speaking to his father through gritted teeth. Part of it was just not wanting to talk right now, which was most of the time. The other part was past hurts where his father was concerned, and it seemed no amount of trying produced true forgiveness on either of their parts.

"I use your old room for my office now, but you can have all of the basement. I finished a kitchen off down there last spring. It's pretty nice. Jack McCormick did the sheetrock. You remember him? He has that farm on Mulvaney Road, the one with the big red barn with the Georgia Bulldogs logo on the roof..."

"Dad! Would you just please... not talk so much." Nash took a long drink of his beer and leaned against the deck railing for support. The doctor had at least gotten him upright after a week in the hospital. But one leg was still in a cast, which meant he spent most of his time in a wheelchair or on crutches. He had other injuries too, and that would require extensive physical therapy now that he was "home".

His father sighed. "I don't know what to say to you."

Nash felt bad. Right now, he didn't want to talk to anyone. He wanted to be mad, drink beer with his pain pills against doctor's orders and just forget everything that had happened to him.

He sighed and eased himself back down into his wheelchair. "I don't think there's much to say, Dad."

Brick stood and walked across the deck, looking out over his six acre property. "This wouldn't have happened if you'd stayed here. You know that, right? I mean, we have a perfect safety record..."

"Dad, this wasn't anyone's fault. Bulls can't be totally controlled. You have to know that better than anyone."

"Nah, they can't be controlled, but I sure as hell never let one step on me. Where was your helper?"

"Don't you start pointing fingers and blaming people. You don't know a damn thing about my crew!"

Ah yes. This felt more familiar. He'd never been good enough for his father, no matter how hard he'd tried. And now he was right back where he'd started - defending himself to the man who'd made his upbringing a living hell.

Brick had provided for his family well. Maybe too well. Nash had had all he ever wanted as a kid. A nice house, vacations to the beach, a four wheeler. The only thing he didn't have was a happy home.

Brick and Nash's late mother, Diane, had fought constantly. His father wasn't physically abusive, but his words had cut deeper than any knife ever could.

Of course, his mother was no dainty flower either. She'd been a hard charging alcoholic who had a worse cussing problem that even the grittiest sailor at any port.

But even she had gotten enough of Brick by the time Nash was twelve, and she'd left. She didn't take her son. Brick gave her enough money, and she'd seen that as her escape. Six months later, Brick had walked into Nash's bedroom and said "Your mother is dead. Funeral is Tuesday" and walked out.

Alcoholism is a lethal disease.

But Nash pressed on, learned how to deal with his father. The only way to connect was to be a rodeo man. Ride those bulls better than anyone else could. Prove himself. Make his father money. Be tougher than he really was.

And he did. He was the best. He'd beat the best many times. But his father's face had never changed. Words of praise had never crossed his lips.

Instead, he'd said things like "Next time, stay on longer. You'll never beat the big guys with a time like that."

One day, when he was sixteen, his life had changed. Someone finally looked at him the way he wanted his father to look at him.

It was at a local youth bull riding expo where he'd first seen her. Blue eyes that lit up even across a dirty bull riding pen in broad daylight. Long, dark hair swept up into a ponytail that swayed back and forth in the most mesmerizing way when she walked. A smile so bright that he was glad he was wearing sunglasses at the time. And she was smiling *at him*.

"You hear me?" Brick said loudly, breaking him out of his biggest happy memory from Whiskey Ridge. His father's voice was like an unwelcome TV commercial interrupting a sappy romance movie.

"What?" Nash closed his eyes and rubbed the bridge of his nose. He just wanted to take a nap.

"Your doctor sent these prescriptions along with Deke. You better get them filled before the pharmacy closes." Brick pulled the small papers from his pocket and tossed them into Nash's lap before walking into the house and slamming the door behind him.

CHAPTER 3

*I*f there was one good thing about a small town, it was the ability to travel around without a vehicle. Nash could only take himself places in his wheelchair since his father's huge truck certainly wasn't handicap accessible, and he was not in any condition to drive anyway.

He hated feeling like he couldn't do things. In a week, he would be starting physical therapy at the hospital three days a week. At least he might start seeing some improvement in his mobility then.

"Nash? Is that you?" he heard a man's voice say from behind him. The bad part of a small town is seeing people you don't want to see, or at least you don't want them to see you when things aren't good. It's much easier to pretend life is grand from across the country.

"Hey, Mr. Jackson. How're you doing these days?" The older man had been a neighbor of theirs when he was growing up. He'd always been kind to Nash, a welcome smile when his father was on his back. Watching Ernest Jackson raise his three boys had been like watching a 1950s TV show, and Nash remembered being so jealous of those boys winning the "father lottery".

"Seems I'm doing a little better than you these days, son. What in the world happened to your leg?"

"Turns out you should never allow a bull to step on you," Nash said, forcing a smile.

"Ouch!"

"Yeah, I said a little more than that when it happened… before I passed out anyway."

The older man smiled. "Well, I'd better get Ellie's medicine home to her. She's got a terrible case of pneumonia. Just got out of the hospital today."

"I'm so sorry to hear that. Please give her my best wishes for a speedy recovery," Nash said as Mr. Jackson opened the door to the pharmacy for him to roll through.

"Will do. And once she's feeling better, I'm sure she'd love to have you over for dinner. Catch up and so forth."

"Sounds like a plan," Nash said, not ever planning to do it but wanting to be nice. The faster he could flee from Whiskey Ridge, the better.

Mr. Jackson smiled and waved one more time before making his way down the sidewalk. The smell of Mountain View Pharmacy hit him before anything else. The old place still smelled the same - a mixture of medication stench and bubblegum flavored ice cream. Yep, the adjoining soda fountain and ice cream bar were still in full swing, just as he remembered it. Whiskey Ridge never changed, it seemed.

"Well, I do declare! Nash Collier! It's been ages since I've seen your handsome face. Come here and give me a hug!"

Oh Lord, he thought. Not Mimi Davenport. Anyone but her.

Mimi had been that girl all through his school years who had a crush on him and wanted the world to know it. Unfortunately, he didn't reciprocate her feelings in the slightest.

Instead, he spent a large portion of his time trying to avoid her at any cost.

"Hey, Mimi," he said softly, not rolling any closer. But she came out from behind the ice cream freezer anyway.

She looked much the same except with about fifty more pounds and a lot more of her bouffant red hair. It was like she'd gotten lost in time somewhere between the 1950s and 1960s even though neither of them were alive back then.

Before he could stop her, she leaned down and gave him a big hug while planting a kiss on his cheek. Why did she smell like hot dogs?

"Soooo… where have you been all these years? Mama told me you were out West until some bull charged at you and crushed you?"

Nash almost laughed at that characterization. Funny how small town gossip could be better than any movie plot.

He was reminded of that game they played in elementary school called "telephone". The teacher would whisper something into the first kid's ear, like "The brown cow likes green grass" and by the time it made it to the end of the row of kids, it was more like "The yellow pigeon eats hamburgers".

"Actually, he didn't charge at me…"

"And you poor thing. Look at your mangled leg. Are you married? Mama said your Daddy has to take care of you now. So sad that you can't compete anymore."

"Well, I don't know for sure if I…"

"And no wife to care for you? Well, sweetie, you let me know if you need anything. I went to massage school, ya know. I can help work out any kinks you need. Oh, look, there's Thelma. Lord knows she'll kill me if I don't go scoop her ice cream. I always give her an extra scoop. Bye bye for now!"

And like some kind of insane whirlwind, she was gone.

Nash sighed and prayed to God that he wouldn't see

anyone else he knew on this little trip. Thankfully, he didn't recognize the teenage boy working the counter.

"Can I help you, sir?"

Sir? Gosh he felt old all of the sudden. The last time he was in Whiskey Ridge, he was the one calling people "sir".

"I'm here to pick up a prescription for Nash Collier."

EMMY FROZE IN PLACE. Did the guy in the wheelchair just say Nash Collier? She couldn't see his face, only the back of his head, but gosh his voice sounded a lot like…

"Honey, do you want whipped cream on that?" Mimi asked from behind the counter, forcing Emmy to return her attention to the banana split she required as an emotional eating crutch today. She'd only wandered into the drug store after seeing Mr. Jackson on the sidewalk. He'd suggested that she take advantage of the sale they were having on banana splits today.

"Um, yes…" Emmy said, turning her head back around to try to catch a glimpse of the man in the wheelchair. Now, a line had formed as the poor teenage boy behind the counter struggled to ring something up.

"What about nuts?"

"What?" Emmy responded as she swung her head back around to look at Mimi.

"Nuts?"

"Who's nuts?" Emmy asked.

Mimi let out a loud laugh, causing numerous people to look their way. Emmy hoped one of those people would be "wheelchair guy", but he was focused on yelling at the cashier for screwing something up.

It couldn't be Nash. She must have mis-heard him. After

all, Nash wasn't in a wheelchair. Well, at least not the last time she saw him over a decade ago.

"We've got pecans, almonds, peanuts..."

When did life get so complicated? Why so many nut choices?

"Peanuts."

"Cherry on top?" Mimi asked, her voice as chipper as a lottery winner on check cashing day.

"Sure. Why not?" Emmy turned again, but wheelchair guy was gone. An old woman with a cane replaced him at the register, and the line had grown longer.

Mimi handed Emmy her banana split and took the five dollar bill that Emmy slid across the counter. She backed up to move out of another customer's way, but her foot caught on something behind her, sending her falling backwards.

Life seemed to move in slow motion, and she waited for the inevitable fall onto the hard tile floor. Instead, she hit something softer. Something that smelled good. Something warm.

It was wheelchair guy's lap.

Embarrassed, she immediately tried to get up, but her banana split was upside down on her lap, and she was quickly losing feeling in areas she couldn't mention in polite company.

"Damn it! What are you doing, woman?" the man yelled. Realizing he had a huge cast on his leg, she felt horrible for hurting him and turned to attempt to get up again.

And then she saw his face.

EMMY. Emmy was sitting on his lap. And if it wasn't for the horrific pain in his leg and arm, and the fact that freezing cold ice cream was numbing his nether regions, he might have had a bodily reaction that wasn't appropriate for public viewing.

"Nash?" she said softly, her blue eyes wide open. He was hyper aware of her smell. Her hair had always smelled like strawberries. Or maybe it was the banana split.

"Emmy?"

She laughed nervously and then looked around. People were staring and most certainly starting the gossip train already.

"I'm so sorry... Let me try to get up..." she continued the nervous laughter as she pushed and pulled until she was on her feet. Without saying anything, she walked to grab a stack of napkins and tried to clean herself up.

"I think you might need to wash those jeans," Nash said with a slight smile. Man, was this uncomfortable.

"I really am sorry. I hope I didn't hurt you too badly."

"You broke my leg. See?" he said, pointing to his cast.

At first, she looked concerned and then realized it was a joke.

Nash maneuvered his wheelchair out of the line of people and over to the side where the bistro tables were. Emmy sat down across from him, still swiping at her pants as Nash used his free hand to flick a stray peanut off his leg.

"Oh, I'm sorry," she said, reaching over and attempting to wipe his pants with the napkins too. It quickly became apparent that he didn't need her touching him any more than was necessary, so he took the napkin from her hand.

"Stop apologizing," he said. "It was an accident. I feel bad that you didn't get your banana split. It was quite... large."

Emmy chuckled. "Yeah, well, emotional eating will do that to a person."

"I didn't know you'd moved back to Whiskey Ridge."

"I didn't. I'm only here temporarily. My mother... well,

let's just say she didn't play well with others at the retirement home so they... kicked her out."

Nash chuckled. "Good old Pauline. Not surprised. Your mom has always been something else."

"I guess that's one way to describe her."

Nash could feel the tension in the air. After all, there was a lot unsaid between them. But more than anything, he couldn't stop looking at her. Memories flooded his brain in a way he never would have expected. First, the good memories. Then, the bad ones. The ones that woke him up at night with the weight of regret for decisions he'd made, things he'd said.

Her eyes hadn't changed. And her mouth, although not smiling a lot, still turned up ever so slightly when she thought something was funny. He expected to see more laugh lines near her eyes after so many years, but they weren't there. A part of him hoped she was using some anti-aging eye cream because the only other alternative was that she hadn't been laughing much. That thought pained him.

"It was nice to see you... I really need to go..." she said suddenly.

"Aren't you going to get another ice cream?"

"No. I think that was God's way of telling me that my thighs don't need it," she said with a half hearted laugh.

"Your thighs look great to me."

Dear God, why did he just say that? He wasn't even on that much medication at the moment.

"What?"

"Sorry. I didn't mean to say..."

"It's okay..."

"This is awkward," Nash admitted. "I didn't expect to see you here, Emmy."

She slowly sat back down and smiled. "I certainly didn't

expect to see you. The last time I heard anything about you, it was some championship in Vegas."

"Yeah, well those days might be over, as you can see." He looked down at his leg and then back at her.

"What happened?"

"My bull stepped on me."

"Jeez, what did you do to him to make him do that?"

He knew she was joking, but he wasn't ready for it to be funny yet. She apparently picked up on that.

"Sorry. Bad joke."

"Stop apologizing."

"Stop telling me what to do, Nash." Ah, there she was, the real Emmy. The one with a stubborn streak a mile long.

"I'm not telling you what to do."

"Sounds like you are, actually. If I want to apologize, I will."

"I'm just saying it's not necessary."

"It's necessary if I feel it is."

This was the dumbest argument he'd ever been a part of.

"Calm down." Oops, wrong thing to say to any woman, but definitely where Emmy Moore was concerned.

She shot up out of the flimsy bistro chair, almost sending it flying out from behind her.

"Some things never change!"

With that, she left the pharmacy and left Nash sitting at the small table alone, trying to figure out yet again how he'd angered Emmy.

"Well, some things sure don't change, huh?" Mimi said, walking up to the table with her hand on her hip.

"Yeah, that's what I've heard."

EMMY STOOD AROUND THE CORNER, out of sight from Nash

and anyone else who might have witnessed their immensely awkward situation.

She'd fallen in his lap.

She'd spilled ice cream and various toppings all over herself and him.

She'd attempted to wipe his crotch with paper napkins like it was a normal thing to do after more than a decade apart.

But worse than all of that was the fact that there were feelings there. Anger. Sadness. Regret. And, if she was honest, a little bit of lust.

Even in a wheelchair, he was still gorgeous. A sharp, chiseled jawbone. Green eyes the color of jade. A little scruff along his jawline. Strong, broad shoulders that had carried her around on more than one occasion in their younger years.

And now he was back in Whiskey Ridge. What were the odds that they'd both find themselves forced into returning home, even if temporarily?

Fate. That's what her cousin, Debbie, would say.

But Emmy didn't believe in fate. She had at one point believed that God had one perfect person for her, but then he chose bulls over her and left town.

So she chose the man she thought was a safer bet. Steve. Rock solid, smart Steve. And then he wasted her life savings and sent her into financial ruin.

Men sucked. That was her new motto. Maybe she'd have a t-shirt made.

"Em? Oh my word! When did you get to town?"

Her cousin Debbie stood there with her hands on her hips, leaning against her compact car. The town square was quaint, and it was nearly impossible for a person to escape notice. Not that she didn't want to see her cousin. They were like sisters, after all.

Debbie got the "normal" mother. Pauline was the black sheep, but her sister Susan was a wonderful woman. She had been a quiet, Christian woman only interested in raising her daughter and doing good in the community. When she'd died six years ago, Emmy lost all hope of having anyone to help her care for Pauline.

"Debbie! Oh my gosh. I just got here a few days ago. I was going to call you…"

Debbie pulled her into a big hug. "Don't you fret, girl. I know you weren't avoiding me. I heard what happened with your Mama. Lord, she's quite a character, isn't she?"

"She's not as funny to me as she seems to be to everyone else," Emmy muttered under her breath.

Debbie poked her bottom lip out and put her hands on each of Emmy's arms. "Why don't we get a cup of coffee and catch up? I have a feeling you've got a lot to tell me?"

Debbie had always been Emmy's confidante. She could tell her anything and expect to get a real, honest answer. Debbie didn't pull any punches, but she was also diplomatic just as her mother had been.

"Okay. But can we go to Moe's?"

"On the other side of town?" Debbie asked, confused. "There's a coffee shop right there… Oh… Wait. Is that… Nash Collier?"

Nash thankfully couldn't see them as he rolled the other direction down the sidewalk, evidently headed back to his father's house.

Emmy cleared her throat. "I guess we can stay here after all."

CHAPTER 4

"So, let me get this straight. Your husband left you holding the bag without any financial nest egg. Your mother got kicked out of the retirement home, forcing you to take care of her here. And, to top it all off, you fell into Nash's lap causing an ice cream explosion all over you and him. Am I missing any updates?"

Emmy sighed. "And my boss called me this morning. I lost my position at the hospital. They can't afford to wait around for me to figure out the situation with my mother."

"Sweetie, I'm so sorry. Is there anything I can do?"

"Wave a magic wand?" Emmy wasn't one to cry a lot, but right now she felt like it might be a good option. Just let the waterworks flow and get it all out. But, as her mother had always reminded her, when the crying was over the problems remained.

"Okay, let's start with the problems one by one."

"Your Mom used to say that," Emmy said with a smile.

"I sure do miss my Momma. She had all the best advice. But she was right. If you look at each problem on its own, it's a lot more manageable."

"None of this feels manageable," Emmy said, taking a sip of her coffee. She stared through the plate glass window of the coffee shop and watched people going about their business.

They looked so happy. So serene. So without problems. But here she sat - going through a divorce with no money, no job, a crazy mother and sticky ice cream between her boobs. How did that nut even get stuck in there?

"Earth to Emmy," Debbie said, waving her hand in front of Emmy's face as she fished the errant nut out of its cleavage hiding spot.

"Sorry. I was just... pondering."

"You've always pondered too much," Debbie said as she opened another sugar package and poured it into her already sugar-laden latte. "Look, this isn't the end of the world. I'll help you as much as I can to get your mother situated, and I know enough people here to get you on at the hospital..."

"I can't take a job here, Deb. That would mean I'm staying. And I'm most assuredly not staying in Whiskey Ridge."

Debbie chuckled and rolled her eyes. "What in the world do you have against this place? It's beautiful, the people are nice, the pace is slow..."

"And the memories are ever-present and not always good..."

"Emmy, it's been more than a ten years since Nash left Whiskey Ridge. You guys had an amazing love story, and then it ended. Why can't you just let it go?"

Emmy bit her lip and leaned her head back. Why couldn't she get over it? She wanted to say it out loud. She wanted to tell Debbie that there was a lot more to what happened with Nash than she had ever told anyone, that there were secrets that only the two of them knew. But she bit her lip hard enough to keep from opening a can of worms she would never be able to close.

"You're right. It's old news, and apparently I'm going to have to deal with Nash for at least a little while. Avoidance is the only tactic I can use now."

～

Nᴀꜱʜ ꜱᴀᴛ in the basement with the dark drapes blocking out any little bit of light that might peek through. Only the TV flickered in the distance with some second-rate 80s movie playing.

He wasn't watching it anyway. Instead, he was staring at his phone, trying unsuccessfully to stop stalking Emmy's social media pages.

He felt like a loser for reading about her life like this, but once he'd seen her it was like the floodgates had opened. He wanted to know more. Where had she been? Was she married? Did she have kids? He pored over every picture like he was trying to solve a puzzle.

Unfortunately, she didn't seem to post a lot of info about her life, and there were only a few older pictures that friends from their high school days had tagged her in.

"Turn some damn lights on down here!" his brother shouted as he descended the stairs. Dang plush carpeting kept Nash from hearing him in time. His brother bumped into the back of the couch, peering over Nash's shoulder before he could stop him. "Emmy? What the hell are you looking at her for?"

Ah, Billy. His father's favorite son, and his pain in the butt older brother.

"I thought you were in Tennessee this week?" Nash said without looking up. Billy fell into the chair next to him and popped open a beer before slamming his dirty cowboy boot up on the coffee table.

"Nah. I finished up my work there this morning. No reason to stick around. Besides, I've got a hot date tonight."

"With?" Nash feigned interest as he continued scrolling through Emmy's posts from two years before.

"Hot blond with big boobs that I met at the bar last weekend. Susie. No, wait. Stella. No… Damn, I can't remember her name."

Billy had always been a player. Even in his thirties, he had no apparent interest in settling down and starting a family. Nash had wanted a family once upon a time. Now he wasn't sure what he wanted, other than to get the heck out of Whiskey Ridge.

"Nice," he said in a monotone voice, hoping his brother would get out of his space sooner rather than later.

"So I ask again, why are you looking at Emmy?"

Nash sighed when it became apparent that Billy wasn't going anywhere. He put his phone back in his pocket. "I ran into her today, that's all."

Billy opened another beer and passed it to Nash. "Dang. Emmy Moore, back in Whiskey Ridge. Never thought I'd see the day. She bolted out of here just about as fast as you did."

"Apparently her mother got kicked out of the retirement home."

Billy let out a big laugh. "I can see that."

Nash finally cracked a smile before downing a swig of beer. "Me too."

"I never understood why ya'll broke up," Billy said offhandedly.

Nash's chest tightened. "Young love doesn't last."

Billy stared at his brother for a long moment. "Yeah, I don't buy it."

"You don't buy what?"

"Man, you were all wound up about that girl, and then

suddenly you split up with her and leave town and never come back. What the hell happened?"

Nash could feel his jaw tightening, even with muscle relaxers surging through his blood. "None of your damn business, Billy."

Billy held up his hands. "Chill out, dude. It was just a question." He stood up and headed upstairs, but not before stopping halfway up. "But let's just say your reaction after all these years speaks volumes."

"WHAT ON GOD'S green earth happened to you?" Pauline asked as Emmy appeared in the kitchen where her mother was sitting, having her regular cup of evening coffee.

"I had a little mishap at the pharmacy." Emmy poured herself a cup of coffee and leaned against the counter.

"Did you fight with Jimbo who drives the ice cream truck?"

"Ha ha ha," Emmy said dryly.

"Go ahead and tell me what happened, Em. You know I'll find out anyhow. Small towns work that way."

Emmy put her mug down on the counter and crossed her arms. "Fine. I ran into Nash."

"And he threw ice cream at you?"

"No, mother, of course not. And it isn't funny. I had no idea he was back in Whiskey Ridge."

"Well, that makes two of us. Never thought I'd see the day he darkened Brick's door again. His daddy is a royal jackass!"

"Mama, please... I already have a headache."

"You have a peanut stuck to your shirt," Pauline pointed out. Emmy wondered if Debbie saw it and just decided it was too funny to point out. "So, you ran into Nash. And then what happened?"

"I fell into his lap while holding a giant banana split."

"His lap? How on Earth did you manage that one?"

"He's in a wheelchair right now. His bull stepped on him."

"Good Lord, this story just keeps on getting better and better," Pauline said with a chuckle as she took a sip of her coffee.

"It's really not funny, mother." Emmy poured out her remaining coffee and rinsed her cup.

"You know, if you'd look at life a little less seriously, I reckon you might be a whole lot happier."

"Point taken. I'm going to get a nice, hot shower. Then I'm going to wrap myself up in my blanket and watch TV on my computer until I pass out."

Emmy started walking up the hallway toward her room. "Sounds like quite a party!" her mother called out to her, the sound of her laughter filling the small house.

~

"EMMY MOORE?" the woman called from behind the counter. Emmy stood, her resume in one hand and her far too large handbag in the other. "Mr. Wayne will see you now."

Mr. Wayne, the head of HR for Whiskey Ridge Hospital, had done a personal favor for Debbie by allowing Emmy to interview. She was sure they had far better applicants for the position she was seeking, but right now she wasn't above using the "it's who you know" excuse. She needed a job, and fast.

Her mounting debt back in Atlanta and the daily calls from collection agencies wasn't helping her mental state at all. On top of that, dealing with her mother's shenanigans and lapses in memory were fraying her already frazzled nerves.

"Hello, Emmy. Nice to meet you," Mr. Wayne said with a

broad smile. He wasn't what she expected. He was young, probably close to her age, and lean with thick brown hair. Her mother would've said he had a "swimmer's build" with his muscular yet wiry frame.

"Nice to meet you too, sir," Emmy said, immediately wanting to take back the sir part. It just didn't feel authentic given their close proximity in age.

"Please, call me David." She nodded before walking past him into the office, taking a seat in the chair across from his very organized desk.

Not much had changed about Whiskey Ridge Hospital in all the years she'd been away. Of course, she had only darkened its doors for the occasional visit to see a sick relative.

Still, the hospital appeared stuck somewhere in time with its dated decor and musty smell.

"I'm glad you could come on such short notice, Emmy. I've heard some great things about you," David said as he took a seat at his desk and straightened his line of pens. One thing was apparent - he had OCD big time. Everything on his desk was at right angles.

"Well, thank you for seeing me so quickly. I know you have a line of people interviewing for this job."

"Jobs are a bit hard to come by around here, but I was impressed by your credentials. Debbie told me you were a physical therapist in Atlanta?"

"Yes. I worked for a private group, but we worked out of one of the largest hospitals there. I really enjoyed it."

"Do you have a specialty?"

"Well, I worked with all types of things. Sports injuries were a big part of our patients, mainly from football teams and a few baseball players. We also worked with car accident victims, although some had to go to the spinal center instead of just regular physical therapy."

"It sounds like you would be more than qualified for this

position. In fact, I'm a little concerned that it wouldn't be challenging enough for you."

"Oh, please don't think that. In fact, I'd welcome a little slower pace."

"I don't mean to pry, Emmy, but can I ask why you would leave such a successful life behind in Atlanta to come back to Whiskey Ridge?"

Emmy swallowed hard. There were so many answers to that question, and none of them were anything she wanted to talk about with a perfect stranger.

"My mother is here, and she needs my help right now." Maybe that would suffice as an explanation as to why she had fled Atlanta.

"Understood. My parents are getting elderly too, but thankfully my brother lives close to them and can help out."

"Yeah, that's great," Emmy said, plastering a fake smile on her face. Right now, she really just wanted to finish the interview, get the job and gorge on the banana split she missed out on a few days ago.

"Well, listen, I don't think there's any reason to beat around the bush. You have the job if you want it."

"Really? Oh, wow. Thanks so much. When do I start?"

"Actually, if you could start tomorrow morning, that would be a big help. We have a backlog of therapy patients that have been traveling to the next town over for care. We're going to keep you very busy, Ms. Moore."

Emmy smiled. "Good. I like to be busy." And right now, being busy was a godsend.

CHAPTER 5

*N*ash rolled into the kitchen after maneuvering himself around the outside of the house, up the walkway to the front door and through the living room. His father's house wasn't exactly handicap accessible.

But thankfully, the house was empty right now, which gave him a little slice of peace. Between listening to his brother prod him with questions about Emmy and his father ridicule pretty much every decision he'd ever made in his life, his mind was a whirlwind of negativity right now.

What he wanted was a nice, cold beer and some uninterrupted time in front of the TV. He pulled on the refrigerator door with his good arm and surveyed what was available to him. Beer was on top, just enough to be out of reach.

"Damn it," he muttered to himself as he inched his way forward on his seat and extended his good arm as far as possible. He managed to topple one of the glass bottles, but it didn't land in his hand. Instead, it bypassed him completely, bounced off the arm rest and shattered against the cold tile floor below.

"What in the holy hell are you doing?" Brick yelled from the front door. Great, he wasn't alone after all.

"Well, ya know, I thought busting a beer bottle all over the damn floor sounded like a fun idea today. I was a little bored," Nash said through gritted teeth. His father pulled the back of his wheelchair away from the towering appliance and slammed the door.

"You've got to start therapy, Nash. You're not getting any better."

"I've decided that therapy isn't going to help me. I just need to rest and heal, and then I'll be our of your hair and back to Vegas where I belong." Nash wheeled himself around the large breakfast bar and out of the way of the glass shards that were scattered across the tile floor. He watched as his father struggled to pick them up.

Brick had back problems from years in the rodeo world, and he wasn't getting any younger. But Nash would never mention either of those issues to his father or risk an all out argument that the neighbors several acres away would hear. In Brick's mind, he was invincible no matter his age or medical ailments.

"Back where you belong, huh?" Brick muttered as he tossed another piece of glass in the stainless steel trashcan at the end of the island, causing the sound of pinging metal to reverberate around the room.

"Vegas is my home, Dad. You know that."

"Vegas is the home you *chose*, Nash. And don't think for one second that I don't know you chose Vegas to get away from me." He stood and opened the refrigerator, pulling out two bottles of beer. He popped the top on one and handed it to Nash.

Brick Collier wasn't an emotional man. He didn't cry. He didn't have heartfelt conversations with anyone, especially Nash. They had butted heads since he could remember. But right now, he seemed softer than Nash remembered.

"I chose to go my own way. I needed to break away from…"

"Me," Brick said, finishing his sentence.

Nash sighed. "I needed to be my own man. Surely you of all people can understand that."

"You know, when I was a kid, I remember my Dad wanting me to come work in his plumbing business. He talked about it all the time. 'Boy, I'm building this business so you never have to worry about money in your life', he would say. And I didn't have the heart to tell him that I didn't want to stick my hand in other people's crap everyday for the rest of my life. When he died, I was seventeen years old. I'd apprenticed for him for two years at that point. He died thinking that I would take the reins of his company and build it even bigger. But as soon as I could sell it off, I did. And I made a profit and built my company." Brick took a long sip of his beer. "I guess I should've felt guilty about not continuing the family business, but I can't say I ever did."

Nash had never heard that story. "So you understand that I needed to do my own thing?"

Brick sighed. "No. I don't."

Nash shook his head. "What? How can you not see it's the same situation?"

"It's not the same situation at all, Nash. My Dad wanted me to do what *he* loved. I only asked you to do what you already loved. And you rejected that."

There was a weighty moment of silence between the two men before Nash's cell phone rang. He hesitated for a moment before looking down, but when he noticed his new doctor's phone number, he knew he had to answer it.

"Sorry. It's Dr. Miller…"

Brick waved his hand. "Take it."

Nash pressed the button to answer it. "Hello?"

"Nash? Dr. Miller here."

Dr. Miller was about as gruff as any person he'd ever met. For a small town doctor, he didn't pull any punches.

"What's up, Doc?" Nash said without thinking about the obvious correlation to a popular cartoon character. He heard the doctor grunt under his breath.

"I understand you haven't begun your therapy yet, Nash. Why is that?"

Nash looked up at his father for moment. Brick got the message and excused himself out to the deck, shutting the door behind him.

"Look, Dr. Miller, I just don't think therapy is going to do a dang thing to heal me any faster. I think what I need is some rest here at my father's house, and then I'll be good as new to head back to Vegas. Plus, I think these anti-inflammatories and pain pills are magical…"

"I told you at your appointment what the rules were, Nash. I will not continue prescribing pain medication to a patient who won't even do the simplest things I suggest. Therapy… early therapy… can mean the difference between a full life or one spent in a wheelchair."

"I understand your suggestions…"

"No, I don't think you do. You're becoming too dependent on the medications, and you're not doing the bare minimum to help yourself. I spoke with Dan Sheffield today."

The name Dan Sheffield was enough to stop Nash in his tracks. For all intents and purposes, Dan was his boss. He owned the whole rodeo company that Nash competed for, so Dr. Miller had certainly caught his attention.

"You spoke to Dan?"

"Yes. He called me this morning for an update on your progress."

"But I talked to him two days ago."

"Yes, and he noted that you were slurring your words and hadn't started therapy yet."

Slurring his words? No way that was true. Dr. Miller was just being dramatic.

"I resent being made to feel like a drug addict. I'm taking these pills as prescribed." In his heart of hearts, he knew he was in dangerous territory. With his mother's history of alcoholism, addiction was a definite possibility for Nash.

"And drinking a few beers along with them, I'd bet," Dr. Miller said. Nash looked down at the bottle in his hand and then surveyed the room, wondering if there were nanny cams watching him or something.

"That's my business," Nash said under his breath.

"Well, you're about to be out of business. The rodeo business anyway."

"Excuse me?"

"Let me lay it out for you, my boy. If you don't show up at therapy tomorrow and every other day scheduled for you, Dan is not going to renew your contract."

"I'm his biggest draw, Doc. No way that's true," Nash said, his stomach starting to lurch.

"Well, Mr. Rodeo Celebrity, you're in your thirties, injured and more than a little cocky, so it's quite possible that some young buck is going to take your place while you're 'recuperating' in your father's house."

Nash hated being wrong. He hated being told what to do. But he loved a challenge, and this was starting to feel like one. He'd show them. He'd go to every therapy appointment and work overtime to get back to his prime. He'd come back better than ever no matter what anybody thought.

"Doc, I'll be there bright and early tomorrow."

～

EMMY LIKED FEELING USEFUL AGAIN. It got her mind off her troubles, at least somewhat. Her cell phone was off and in her purse, keeping the collectors at bay. Debbie had offered to sit with Pauline for a few hours, which gave Emmy comfort that her mother wasn't setting the house on fire or something.

"How're you feeling, Mrs. Riley?" Emmy asked the older woman who was her first therapy patient of the day. She had a bad back and mostly just needed some trigger point massage and heat packs.

"Oh, I'm good, dear," she said, though her voice was muffled as she lay face down on the table.

"Good. My next patient is due in soon, but Hillary will help you once your timer goes off, okay?" Hillary was Emmy's assistant, a young college student studying physical therapy. She was good and did what Emmy asked of her, although she was a bit shy so they needed to work on that.

"Ms. Moore?" Hillary said as she walked into the therapy area.

"Again, please call me Emmy. Okay?" She smiled through semi-gritted teeth. Emmy wasn't one who liked repeating herself. And being called "Ms" made her feel ancient.

"Sorry. Um, your next patient is here. Should I bring him back?"

"Yes, please. I need to run to the restroom, so just put him in the evaluation area and I'll be there shortly. And be sure to ask if he'd like some water or coffee."

"Yes, ma'am."

Ma'am. Ugh.

Emmy stood in the small bathroom and stared at herself in the mirror. It was barely past nine in the morning and she already looked haggard. She was mentally exhausted between living with her mother and worrying about money.

Maybe she could afford some new makeup to hide the dark circles under her eyes.

She walked back out into the therapy area and saw Hillary working with Mrs. Riley. The older woman waved at her as she stood and stretched her back.

"If that stiffens up, try an ice pack for twenty minutes followed by a heating pad for twenty minutes, okay?" Emmy called to her.

She turned to go into the evaluation room, a small area off the large therapy room. She wasn't expecting to see Nash sitting there, a scowl on his face.

"Good morning," she said. He looked up and stalled for a moment before speaking.

"Hey. I mean good morning. What're you doing here?"

Emmy laughed. "I work here. I'm a physical therapist."

"Oh my gosh…"

"You didn't know that?"

"Of course not. I would've requested…" he said, before stopping himself.

"Someone else? Nice vote of confidence." She turned toward the desk and picked up an iPad that had all of her patient files and notes in it.

"I didn't mean it that way. It's just that this is stressful enough…"

Emmy sat down and looked at him with her best poker face. "I'm a professional, Nash. I've worked in physical therapy for a long time. And I assure you that our past… issues… won't hamper my ability to treat you. Are we clear?"

"Yes, ma'am," he said with a sly smile.

"Don't call me ma'am."

"So how long is this going to take?" he asked, leaning his head back and closing his eyes.

"About an hour, I would think."

"No. I mean this whole therapy thing. I need to get back to Vegas."

"Ah, yes, Vegas. Your holy land. Well, I wouldn't want to keep you any longer than necessary." She looked down at the iPad, her vision blurry from irritation.

"Hey, I thought you said we wouldn't have any issues relating to our past?"

"Fine. Sorry. Small slip-up. Won't happen again."

"You still didn't answer me."

"That's because I don't know, Nash. Everyone responds differently to treatment. You're young, so that's in your favor."

"You think I'm young?" he asked with a smile.

"We're almost the same age, Nash."

He sighed. "Ballpark? How long are we looking at?"

She looked at his chart. "Dr. Miller wasn't overly optimistic in his notes."

"He hates me."

"Regardless, he noted that you're taking painkillers and anti-inflammatory medications?"

"Yes. When a bull steps on you, it tends to hurt."

She looked up and smiled slightly. "I'm sure it does."

"Is there anyone else? Literally, anyone?"

"Anyone else for what?"

"To be my therapist."

Emmy had to admit that his words hurt. Either he didn't trust her or he hated her, and both options bothered her more than she'd like to admit.

"No. I'm all you've got around here, Nash." She turned off the tablet and looked at him. "But I will promise you this - If you'll do what I ask and show up to therapy, I will give you one hundred percent of my knowledge. I will study case histories and try to find even more information to help you. I will do everything I can to get you back on your feet and back to the job you love as soon as possible. I'll work with you and not let our past interfere at all. Deal?"

Nash looked up, his eyes softening a bit. He smiled. "Deal. And thank you, Emmy. I really do appreciate it."

She sucked in a ragged, but thankfully quiet, breath. "It's no problem. It's what I do for all of my patients."

She couldn't be sure, but his face seemed to fall a bit at the thought that he wasn't special. He was just another patient that she would tend to as best she could.

The only problem was, he was special.

CHAPTER 6

*E*mmy sat across from her cousin, whose face was full of surprise.

"He's your patient?" she said, stifling the giggle that was sure to erupt at any moment.

"Yes. And nobody was as surprised as I was. I mean I guess I should've known that he needed to have physical therapy while he was here, but I haven't exactly been thinking clearly lately."

Debbie picked her cinnamon bun apart, licking the sticky cinnamon mixture off her thumb before continuing. "How do you feel about this?"

"Well, it definitely isn't my first choice, but I have to be a professional. I certainly can't afford to lose this new job. Plus, the faster I can get him up and running, the faster he'll leave Whiskey Ridge."

"Are you sure you want him to leave?" Debbie asked, barely making eye contact, a quirk of a smile playing across her lips.

"And just what is that supposed to mean?"

"I think you know what it means. You two certainly have a history. I mean, do you think there's a future?"

Emmy barely let the words leave Debbie's mouth before interrupting her. "Are you crazy? You should know better than anyone else about our history. I certainly don't want to step into that again. I have absolutely no romantic interest in Nash. He's my patient. That's all."

"Okay, if you say so."

"Well I say so. Now, if you'll excuse me, I have to get to work. My first patient is coming in about twenty minutes."

"Is it Nash?" Debbie asked, chuckling under her breath.

"No. For your information, it's a new patient. A *female* patient."

Emmy stood up and pinched her cousin's of her arm, causing her to wince. "Don't forget that I have the meanest pinches in all of Georgia."

Debbie laughed as she rubbed her arm.

NASH SAT on the back deck overlooking his father's yard. There were few places on Earth as peaceful as Whiskey Ridge, but the thought of ever calling it home again was foreign to him. He'd gotten used to his life out in Vegas, although the hectic pace sometimes wore him down. The last thing he wanted to have happen was to turn into his father – becoming an old man and being alone. But he needed to keep his mind occupied because otherwise it would wander to memories that he'd rather forget.

Still, there were times that he wished he had another life. A quiet place to call home. A wife who loved him and little kids running around underfoot. But he'd made a conscious decision to give the possibility of that life up many years ago, and he certainly wasn't going back now.

He loved his career, plus it was the only thing he knew how to do. From the very youngest age, it had been his life. Even before he wanted it to be his life, he had been thrust into the world of rodeo and bull riding by his father.

He could vividly remember his father on the phone day and night trying to build his company. Talking about all of the money he made. Talking about the day that Nash would take over. But that didn't seem likely to happen now either.

And even though he didn't like to think about it, his memories had always been the true enemy. Visions of Emmy standing in the orange Georgia clay in her dusty cowboy boots, watching him learn the ropes of the rodeo business.

Thoughts of sweet kisses behind the barn.

Thoughts of hotter kisses behind the bales of hay in the loft of the very same barn.

Thoughts of mistakes made and promises not kept.

His memories were all so muddled up, and the pain pills certainly weren't helping. He would have to withdraw from those soon, no matter how much his body hurt. He wasn't going to become addicted like his mother.

His phone buzzed in his pocket, shaking him out of yet another walk down memory lane. Whiskey Ridge seemed to do that to him.

"Hello?"

"Hey, man! How're you feeling?"

The unmistakable voice of his friend, Deke, was on the other end of the line. He had to admit it was good to hear from him, but he was jealous. Deke was currently living the life he wanted to get back to.

"Hanging in there. How's it going out there?"

"Well, I'm out in Texas this week. We've got a big championship on Saturday, you know."

Nash went silent for a moment. That had always been one of his favorite championships of the year. And he should be there. But instead he was sitting in a wheelchair like some sort of crippled old man.

"Yeah, I know. Who did Dan put in my place?"

"I didn't call to talk about that."

"Deke, I'm asking you a question."

Deke went quiet on the line for a moment before answering. "Travis."

Nash groaned under his breath. "Travis Blake? Seriously. That kid won't win a damn thing!"

"He's been winning a lot lately, Nash. Dan thinks he can take this thing."

"Oh, please. How old is he, nineteen?"

"He's twenty-two, and he's got a lot of promise, man. He's a good kid…"

"What are you? The president of his fan club?"

Deke chuckled. "How's therapy going?"

"I just started yesterday, so I'm almost all healed," Nash said sarcastically.

"Yesterday? What was the hold up?"

Nash leaned back against the log chair he'd lowered himself into. "Just wasn't ready to start yet."

"Come on, man. I know you. Why were you procrastinating?"

"Just hoped I could get better without it, I guess."

"Yes, because just sitting around taking pain pills is known to magically repair tendons and muscles."

"Don't be a jackass, Deke."

"I'm not the jackass in this situation, Nash. If you want to come back and give Travis a run for his money, you're going to have to get off the pills and throw yourself into therapy. You have to know that."

Nash sighed. "I know that."

"Good. Then attack therapy like you attack your job. Therapy *is* your job until you can get back to the ring."

Nash knew his friend was right. He needed to ditch the pills and put his full effort into therapy or he might never get back to his life. And that was just what he was going to do. Emmy or not, he was going into therapy tomorrow like a champion.

~

EMMY WAS NOT A MORNING PERSON. These new hours, seeing patients as early as 7 am, were getting to her already. She'd talked to the receptionist about scheduling her easier patients before ten, just to give herself a little time to amp up with coffee.

But today she was keenly aware that her first patient was Nash. Her hardest, most complicated patient for a variety of reasons.

Certainly, Nash's medical case was complicated all by itself, but the feelings and emotions from their past didn't make things any easier.

When she looked at him, she saw so many things. His gorgeous honey brown eyes that still had those hints of hazel green in them, even though crows feet - a sexy thing on any man as far as she was concerned - were starting to form around his eyes.

She saw his sun tinted brown hair, still thick and wavy like it was when they were young. She'd loved watching his hair bounce around and blow in the wind when he rode bulls, the Georgia clay dust kicking up into the air.

But she also saw other things when she looked at Nash Collier. Pain. Tears. The back of his Mustang as he drove it out of Whiskey Ridge and left her in that orange plume of dust.

Sometimes she wondered where it had all gone wrong,

but she couldn't linger in that space. If she did, her whole day would be shot and she'd get nothing done.

Their relationship, and its ultimate demise, was like a big un-solvable math problem. And she obviously wasn't great a math or she wouldn't be living back in Whiskey Ridge with a financial mess waiting for her back in Atlanta.

"Good morning," Nash said as she approached, her first cup of coffee starting to make its way through her veins.

"Morning. Ready to get started?" she asked, trying not to make eye contact. That wasn't going to work since physical therapists needed to actually look at their patients in order to help them. She had to get past these jumbled up feelings.

"I'm ready to rock this," he said, a weird grin on his face. For a moment, she worried that he was taking something other than pain pills.

"Are you okay?"

"Of course I am. Why?"

"You seem a little... revved up this morning."

Nash chuckled. "I'm just ready to get back to my life, Emmy. I'm here - at your mercy - to put in my full effort no matter what you throw at me. I need to get better fast."

Emmy sighed and sat on the edge of the massage table across from Nash's wheelchair.

"Nash, this isn't a tournament or a championship. You have no idea how your body is going to respond to treatment. And if you try to force it, you might just put yourself out of commission permanently."

"Why do you have to be so damn negative all the time?" he said, rolling his eyes.

"I'm not being negative. I'm being realistic. But you never were one for being realistic, were you?" she shot back, regretting her words immediately.

"Emmy..."

"Sorry. It's hard to separate the past from the present.

Won't happen again. Okay, let's get started, shall we?" Emmy stood up and started preparing the table.

"We shall."

She shot him a glance and decided not to respond to his sarcastic comment.

"First, I'm going to help you up onto the table so that I can go over your injuries and see what we're starting with." She reached out her hand to help him up, but Nash ignored it and started to stand up on his own.

"I've got it," he mumbled.

"Of course you do," she mumbled back. They'd always been like this, one upping each other, always needing to get the last word.

Nash eased himself over to the table and gingerly leaned back enough to get his butt over the edge.

"At least let me help you scoot back," Emmy said without waiting for a response. He winced as she helped him, eventually lying down onto the pillow behind him.

"You can just relax. I'm going to look over Dr. Miller's notes about your injuries and then do some assessments, okay?"

"Have at it," Nash said, acting cool as he always did. His motto was "never let them see you sweat", and he'd always taken that approach to life and relationships.

"Okay, do you feel any pain here?" Emmy asked as she started pressing on different areas of his injured leg.

"Nope."

"What about here?" Before he could answer, Nash almost jumped off the table. "Okay, I'll take that as a yes…"

"What the hell did you do?" he asked, his eyebrows furrowed together.

"I touched your muscle that's injured."

"Are you trying to hurt me?"

"Of course not, Nash. This is my job. We have to find the source of the pain and treat it."

"Well, you found it."

Emmy struggled not to giggle. "You can relax. I'm not going to press it like that again today. Now, I'm going to start working out some of the kinks and see if we can get more mobility in this leg."

"Okay…"

Emmy pulled some lotion off the shelf and rubbed it into her hands, completed aware that Nash was watching her closely.

She began rubbing her hands across his thigh muscle first, his well toned legs reminding her of times gone by.

Nash had amazing legs, even if they were injured at the moment. He had to have strong legs to hold onto the back of a bull, of course.

And right now, running her hands across the thigh of the man she'd loved more than anyone else so many years ago was pure torture. She knew those legs. She'd touched them so many times in her life, and this felt like coming home again.

She needed to distract herself. She started thinking other things in her mind like her grocery list, her mother's podiatry appointment coming up for that ingrown toenail she had… But it wasn't working. She was keenly aware that she was touching Nash's thigh. God help her when she had to work on his glutes soon.

OH GOD. Emmy was touching his thigh. It felt wrong. It felt right. It felt weird. He wanted to run but if he could do that, he wouldn't need physical therapy in the first place.

They locked eyes for a moment as she rubbed the muscles

of his calf now. He quickly closed his eyes trying to avoid an embarrassing situation. And the situation could get a lot more embarrassing if he didn't distract himself soon. He was wearing pretty tight shorts after all. And he was basically on full display. Gosh, why didn't she have him lay face down?

As he settled into the rhythm of her touch, his mind started to wander back to the days when her touch was always welcome.

They'd just been young teenagers when they first met at the rodeo. She was there with friends, and he was just learning the ropes of his family business.

But once he'd seen her across the ring, nothing else mattered. It was like a lightning bolt, just like in those sappy romantic movies.

He knew immediately that she was special. And when she'd smiled at him, all bets were off.

Emmy had gone to the same high school, but their paths hadn't really crossed much up until that point. She was a straight A student who hung out with the serious, AKA "nerdy", crowd mostly. A member of the chorus and French club, Emmy wasn't really someone who would've hung around Nash.

He was more on the wild side, jumping out of barn lofts and asking to tame wild horses. He had no filter, no way to turn off his need for adrenaline. And his father loved that about him, urging him into the rodeo world as soon as possible.

Billy had always worked in the rodeo too, but not as a competitor. He was too absent minded and had little common sense, not a great combination when riding a two-thousand pound very angry animal.

So Brick had groomed Nash from a young age to take over the business one day. And when he saw Nash take an interest in Emmy, he wasn't having any of it.

"Women only tie you down, boy. Don't fall for the pretty little package," was about the extent of Brick's relationship advice to his sons. Billy had stuck to it, even all these years later. But Nash hadn't, something he'd kicked himself for over the years.

Why couldn't he have just not cared so much about Emmy? Why had he fallen in love with her so hard?

Those weren't the only questions he'd asked himself over these years. He'd both beat himself up for loving her and leaving her. Each one, in his mind anyway, had equally messed up his life.

"Is this pressure okay?" she asked, her voice soft. He opened his eyes quickly, almost sure she could read his mind and know he was thinking about her, about their past.

"What? Oh. Yeah. It's fine."

She looked at him, her head cocked a bit for a moment, and then went back to her work.

Emmy looked the same really. Same long hair that she kept tucked behind one ear most of the time. Same sea blue eyes that danced when she laughed, although he hadn't seen much of that lately.

But she was different at the same time. More reserved. More defensive. He had to wonder how much of that was his fault. Maybe she didn't trust people because of how their worlds split apart all those years ago. And then he'd left her to pick up the pieces alone.

"Okay," she said, breaking up his thoughts, "Let's have you turn over so I can work on some other areas..."

HE'D BEEN LOOKING at her. What was he thinking? Was he remembering their past together like she was? Or was he simply wishing he was back in Vegas with all of the beautiful women he surely attracted out West?

"Does this hurt?" she asked as she eased her fingers into the back of his thigh, trying desperately not to look at his super toned butt that was hidden just under the khaki fabric of his shorts.

"No. It actually feels good," he said, his voice muffled by the massage table.

This was torture. She was so conflicted by feelings that she was finding it hard to do her job already. How was she going to survive several weeks of this?

But she had to. There were no other choices. She was a professional, and asking not to work with a specific patient just because they'd dated in high school would make her look like an idiot in front of her new boss.

If only he'd just been her high school sweetheart. But it had been a whole lot more. And it had been way more complicated. She knew it, and Nash knew it.

The air of tension between them was thick, and she could only hope that would get better with time. And then he'd been on his merry way back to Vegas, and she'd... Well, she had no idea what she would be doing by then. Her life was a mixed up mess right now.

After fifteen minutes, Emmy couldn't take it anymore and helped Nash sit up.

"Let's work on this arm," she said, putting more cream on her hands. He held his arm out, and she rested it on a thick foam pad as she started to work it.

"So, your mom got kicked out of the retirement village, huh?" Nash finally said, obviously trying to make small talk.

"Yep. I was so proud," she said, unable to stifle a sarcastic laugh.

"Good old Pauline..."

"I just don't find her as amusing as everyone else."

"You never did, Emmy."

"Are you saying I don't have a good sense of humor?" she asked, looking at him with a hint of a smile.

"Not saying that at all. You just never understood your mother."

"Oh, and you did?"

Nash laughed. "More than you did. She got me."

"That's because neither of you has a filter between your brain and mouth, and you both have impulse control problems."

Ah, now this felt more natural.

"Impulse control problems? How so?"

"You ride bulls, Nash."

"Not impulsively. I trained for years to do what I do."

Emmy realized they were getting back into personal territory and tried to steer the conversation back to his treatment.

"I think this muscle will respond quicker to therapy than your leg. Doesn't seem to be nearly as tender."

"Don't try to distract me from what we were talking about, Em."

Em. He'd always called her that.

"I mean Emmy. I mean, doctor… What should I call you?"

"Emmy is fine."

"Got it. Emmy." She tried not to smile, but it didn't work. Actually, she thought she might have even blushed a bit, but Nash didn't seem to take notice. "Is Pauline just being herself or is something else going on?"

"Well, they say she has some form of early dementia. She has had some episodes of forgetfulness, which is how she ended up at the retirement village in the first place. Kept leaving things in the oven, losing her keys. Stuff like that."

Nash cocked his head to the side for a moment. "This may

be a longshot, but have you asked the doctor to check her vitamin B12?"

Emmy stared at him for a moment, her hands stopping. "What?"

Nash chuckled. "I realize I'm no doctor, but there was this guy who competed on the circuit with me a few years back. His mother started having issues. They said Alzheimer's or something. Anyway, he had money so he got her in to see some fancy, alternative doc out in California. Turned out she was severely low in B12. Started taking these shots, and she was like a new woman from what he said. You may want to just ask, that's all. I could be totally wrong."

Emmy smiled gratefully. "Thank you, Nash. Really. I'll look into that. I'd love to think it's something simple like that because the thought of my mother losing her memory…" She stopped for a moment to keep her eyes from welling. "Well, I just don't want that for her."

Nash reached for Emmy's hand, but she quickly pulled back and went back to her work.

CHAPTER 7

*E*mmy sat at the cafeteria table. The hospital wasn't exactly state of the art, and the cafeteria still looked like something out of the 1970s. But the people she worked with were nice, and the food wasn't all that gag inducing as she'd feared. Still, she was going to start bringing her own lunches from now on because the mound of meat on her plate didn't have enough gravy to cover the strange taste.

"Hey, Emmy!"

Emmy looked up to see one of the nurses she'd befriended since starting at Whiskey Ridge Hospital. Her name was Tara, and she was as bubbly as anyone Emmy had ever met.

With bright blue eyes, a huge toothy smile and a head full of the craziest brown curls she'd ever seen, Tara was a ball of energy. She looked more like she belonged at an art studio than a hospital, but patients seemed to love her sunny personality.

"Hey, Emmy. How's your day going?" she asked as she pointed at the open seat across from Emmy.

"Please join me," Emmy said. "And is there any chance you can identify this?"

Tara leaned over and looked at Emmy's plate. "Well, they claim it's Salisbury steak, but I think it's yesterday's leftover meatloaf with the ketchup scraped off and some gravy added. And I think the gravy is actually the French onion soup thickened with corn starch."

Emmy laughed. "Wow. That was oddly specific."

"I went to culinary school for awhile," Tara said, taking a bite of her salad.

Emmy could totally see that making sense. "Why did you stop?"

"It's weird, really. I had always wanted to be a chef, ever since I was a little kid. But then my grandmother got sick when I was about twelve. She had cancer. I spent a lot of time at the hospital, and I just felt pulled in that direction, you know? I wanted to help people."

Emmy took a sip of her sweet tea. "I totally understand. I think most people who work in medicine consider it a calling."

"I love it. It makes me happy to get up in the morning. So, how's your new job going?"

"Good. I mean, I like my patients. Most of them…"

"Uh oh. That sounds like trouble. Care to explain?"

"Maybe one day," Emmy said with a chuckle. "Listen, I have a question you might know the answer to."

"Sure. What is it?"

"Is it possible for someone to be diagnosed with dementia or Alzheimers but they really have a vitamin B12 deficiency?"

"Absolutely. Why?"

"Well, let me tell you about my mother…"

~

"WHAT IN THE hell are you doing?" Billy asked when he came around the corner and saw Nash laying on the sofa with one arm stretched out to the side and his eyes closed.

"I'm working on my stretches. Emmy said to do this twice a day."

Billy snickered. "Oh, Emmy said so…"

Nash opened his eyes and glared at his brother. "Really? You sound like a ten year old."

"Hey, that ain't a jab. I'd love to go back to being ten years old. Remember Susan Kramer? I kissed her down by the creek when I was that age."

Nash rolled his eyes. "You realize you're the only one who remembers that, right?" He slowly sat up and leaned back against the couch.

"I bet Susan remembers it," Billy said with a grin. "Want a beer?"

"No thanks."

"Oh, did Emmy tell you no beer?"

"Ha ha. Very funny. No, actually my doctor and my boss told me no beer with my medication. But I'm ditching the meds soon too."

"Good because it isn't nearly as much fun to pick at you when you're all drugged up." Billy popped the top on the beer and fell into the arm chair, his cowboy booted legs flung over the arm.

"Can I help you?" Nash said.

"Nope. Dad said to meet him here. He wanted to talk to us."

"Oh great. This feels like the old days."

"Yeah, when he would yell at us for not cleaning up the garage or sucking at bull riding?"

"Or when we didn't cut the grass in straight lines," Nash added. "Pretty much anything we did, or didn't do, resulted in a long lecture about our mutual suckiness."

Billy laughed and took a long drink of his beer. "He's actually changed a good bit in the last few years, Nash. Gotta give him some credit for that."

"I wouldn't know."

"Well, that's because you never come home. He's mellowed a lot since…"

"You boys here?" Brick called from the front door.

"We're here," Nash called back, wondering what his brother had been about to say before they were interrupted.

"Billy, help me with these bags," Brick said. Billy hopped up from the chair and trotted over to the front door.

"What's all that?" Nash asked as he watched his father and brother maneuver several overfilled brown paper bags through the foyer and into the kitchen.

"Just hold your horses," Brick said. "I'll explain in a minute."

Once everything was put away, Billy plopped back into the chair and Brick sat on the stone hearth across from Nash. The living room of his house really was beautiful with floor to ceiling windows overlooking the mountains that stretched out further than he could even see.

"How was therapy?" Brick asked as he took a long drink of a bottle of water.

"It was therapy. Not much to tell. What's this all about, Dad?"

Brick sighed, took another drink and looked at Nash.

"I'd like to introduce you to someone at dinner tonight."

"Who?"

"Her name is Lana."

"Okay… and who is she?"

Brick shot a glance at Billy, who nodded at his father to continue.

"What's the big secret here?" Nash asked.

"Lana is… my fiancee, Nash."

Nash's mouth dropped open as he stared at his father for a moment. Of all the people in the world - well, with the exception of Billy - Brick was the last person he ever expected to get married.

Brick had long ago said that he would never marry again. No way, no how. He was focused on the rodeo business, and a woman would only get in the way of that.

And now he was engaged?

"When did this happen?"

"A couple of weeks before you came back to Whiskey Ridge."

"And why am I just now learning about it?"

"Well, I didn't want to complicate this whole situation, for one thing. Plus, Lana has been out in Colorado visiting her sister so it was easier. But you're still here, and she's home so…"

"So you had to tell me?"

"Well, yeah. Kind of. And I want you to get to know her, Nash. Billy has known her for almost two years now."

"Two years?" Nash said a little louder than he'd planned. "Why didn't you ever tell me about her?"

"Come on, Nash. You know we've barely spoken in the last few years. I didn't think you'd want to hear about my love life."

"First of all, please don't say 'love life' because that creeps me out. And second of all, you didn't think your own son would care that you're getting married?"

Brick thought for a moment. "No, I actually didn't."

"Wow. That's just great. Says a lot about our relationship."

"Come on, man. You're at much as fault as he is," Billy said.

"Seriously? You were raised with this man too, Billy. Maybe you didn't run as soon as you could, but for me it was necessary."

Nash looked at his father, and the hurt was there in his eyes. His stomach clenched when he realized what he'd just said.

"Dad, I shouldn't have…"

"Stop. I don't want to go down this road, Nash. There's plenty of blame to go around, and I accept my fair share of it. But I won't sit in my own house and listen to you try to blame me for your messed up life. You made choices, and I was here when you needed me. I've never abandoned you, and I've been here waiting for you to come home for years. But you chose not to be in my life all those years ago."

"And you chose to shun me because I made a different choice than what you wanted. You made me an outcast in my own family because I wanted to strike out on my own."

"Oh, that's BS and you know it! You and I both know why you left, Nash Collier. And it wasn't just me."

Brick stood up and walked to the kitchen. Billy looked at his brother. "What's he talking about?"

"None of your business," Nash said as he pulled himself up and into his wheelchair.

"Where are you going?" Brick asked from the kitchen. Nash continued rolling toward the side door. Thankfully, his father had installed a temporary ramp for his wheelchair, although he hoped to graduate to full time crutches soon.

"Out."

"Dinner's at seven," Brick yelled back, but Nash said nothing.

~

"I'll take six of the blueberry and six of the chocolate explosion," Emmy said to the girl behind the counter of Mountain View Muffins. The new shop was all the buzz around town, and Emmy had already been there more than once.

"We only have five of the blueberry left, darlin'. You want to try the new caramel nut?"

"Sure," Emmy said, secretly crying inside as she grieved the loss of one of her prized blueberry muffins. Going into the weekend without enough muffins could prove to be disastrous.

"Hungry?"

As she walked out the door, she found Nash sitting at one of the small bistro tables lining the sidewalks of Whiskey Ridge square.

"Are you stalking me?"

"Yes, I'm quite the stalker with my two maimed limbs and squeaky, old man wheelchair."

Emmy couldn't help but laugh at that, but Nash looked super serious and almost upset about something.

"You okay? Are you in pain or something?"

"I'm in the same amount of pain I was this morning. My therapist might not be qualified."

"Very funny," Emmy said as she sat down at the table. "What's going on?"

"Are you a psychologist too?"

Emmy knew Nash well enough to know to change the subject, at least temporarily. He wasn't one to give up information easily.

"Talked to my mom's doctor today about the B12. He's going to test her next week. So thanks for the idea."

"You're welcome. Might not help, but at least it's worth a try."

"Definitely," Emmy said. A long pause hung in the air between them, almost as thick as the caramel on the muffins in her bag. "Okay, what's going on, Nash?"

"Nothing. Listen, I gotta go…"

"No. Come on. You helped me. Now let me help you."

"You helped me this morning," he said with a quirk of a smile.

"Oh, so you're saying I *am* a good physical therapist?"

"What do you have in that bag anyway?"

Emmy held up the bag and acted like she was modeling it. "Well, what I have in here is what you call a 'sugar coma' complete with chocolate and caramel… and blueberries because they're healthy, right?"

Nash finally laughed. "You always did love sugar."

"It's my one vice. Want one?" She didn't really want him to say yes.

"How about we split one?"

"Okay," she said, trying not to show the disappointment in her face. "Pick your poison."

Emmy held out the bag and Nash peered down into it. "Let's go for chocolate."

She pulled one of the muffins out of the bag along with a couple of napkins and split it in half.

"Don't spoil your supper," she said with a smile.

"Don't remind me," Nash said, rolling his eyes before taking a bite.

"Did I hit a nerve? I thought supper was a pretty safe topic."

"It's my Dad."

Emmy stilled for a moment and struggled to keep her face neutral. Brick had never been her biggest fan, and she definitely wasn't his.

"Your father?"

"He announced to me today that not only has he been seriously dating some woman named Lana for two years, but they're engaged. And he wants me to meet her tonight at dinner."

"Ohhhh… That explains the look and the mood and the need for chocolate."

"No, I need hard liquor but I don't want to lose my job."

"Chocolate is safer."

"I guess."

"Listen, Nash. I've never been your father's biggest proponent, but everyone deserves to fall in love. Maybe he finally found the person who can…"

"Put up with him?"

"Well, I wasn't going to say that exactly."

"But you were thinking it," Nash said, smiling as he devoured the last large bite in one move.

"A lady doesn't speak ill of others."

Nash let out a deep laugh at that one. "You still have that dry wit, Emmy Lou Moore."

She'd always loved when he said her full name. Something about the intimacy of that took her back to their high school days sitting at the ice cream shop talking about life for hours until the street lights came on. Those were simpler times.

"Hello? You in there?" Nash asked, waving his good hand in front of her face.

"Oh, yeah. Sorry. I was just thinking."

"About?"

"Nothing really."

"Nope. Not fair. I spilled my guts. Now it's your turn."

"Fine. I was just remembering the old days at Libson's Ice Cream Shop."

"Man, you really are a sugar-holic!"

Emmy threw a wadded up napkin at his face as he ducked out of the way.

"Those were good times, don't you think?"

Nash sat for a moment, looking at her carefully. "Most of them. Some not so good."

"Well, that's life," she said, sitting back and sighing.

"Why are you here, Emmy?"

"I thought we were clear that it was the sugar that brought me here?"

"No. I mean why are you back in Whiskey Ridge?"

She went silent for a moment, trying not to look him in the eye. Nash could always tell when she was lying.

"I told you I came back because of my mother."

"Yes, and I know that's partly true. But that isn't all of it, Em. Tell me."

"Nash, I don't think this is a good idea..." she said, starting to stand up.

"You were my whole world back then."

"What?" she said, slowly sitting back down.

"You were everything. And we were friends once, even before we started getting serious. I knew you better than I knew myself."

"Your point?"

"There's no one else you can talk to about whatever is going on that will understand it like I do."

"You're awfully full of yourself, Nash Collier."

He grinned. "And that surprises you?"

"Actually, no."

"Tell me."

She bit both of lips and then took in a deep breath.

"I'm in the middle of divorcing my cheating husband who stole my life savings from me."

Nash's eyes grew wide, almost like he didn't know what to say.

Emmy continued. "I heard from my attorney today, and our divorce is being fast-tracked but I'll basically be left in financial ruin once this is all over."

"What a freaking jackass. You know, I know some people in Atlanta. Want me to make a call?"

"Nash! I don't want him killed!"

Nash chuckled. "Fine. But if we scared him enough to get him to at least run into the ring with a certain bull…"

"Stop. That's not funny."

Nash stopped talking for a moment and then reached across the table and put his hand over Emmy's.

"Look, I don't know who this guy is, but he obviously didn't appreciate what he had."

"You don't have to try to make me feel better, really."

"I'm not trying to make you feel better. I'm just saying that if I had another chance…"

He yanked his hand back and avoided eye contact for a moment.

"What did you say?"

"Nothing. Must be the drugs. Or the chocolate. Look, I gotta go. My Dad expects me for dinner and so forth…"

He started trying to back up from the table, but his wheel was stuck.

"Let me help you," Emmy said, standing up.

"No, no, it's fine. I've got it. Listen, thanks for the muffin. And I'll see you Monday, okay?"

Before Emmy could say another word, Nash was quickly wheeling himself down the sidewalk toward his father's house. And Emmy was left to wonder what had just happened.

CHAPTER 8

"*N*ash, this is Lana. Lana, this is my long lost son, Nash."

Nash stared at the woman. She was a far cry from what he'd expected. She was professional looking with shoulder length black hair, very minimal makeup and a welcoming smile.

"Nice to meet you," Nash said.

"Oh, Nash, I'm so happy to finally meet you. Your father is so proud of you."

Proud? His father. Surely she had him confused with someone else.

Brick was on the back deck working the grill with Billy while Nash got acquainted - albeit awkwardly - with his soon to be new step mother.

"Proud? Of me?"

"Of course, sweetie. He's talked about you in such glowing terms since I met him. I couldn't wait to meet you!" She continued chopping the lettuce for the salad, tossing each piece into a large colander in the sink.

"Wow. That's interesting. I'm not sure he told you the full story…"

"Sure he did. Honey, family stuff can be hard. I have a grown daughter, and we didn't speak for six months because of a stupid argument. These things happen. But your Daddy was proud of you even when he didn't agree with your choices."

"Good to hear… I guess…"

Nash was having problems processing all of the information he was getting lately. His father's engagement. Emmy's cheating, stealing husband.

Things had changed a lot in Whiskey Ridge, it appeared.

"So how did you meet my father?"

Lana smiled as she started shredding purple cabbage over the bowl.

"Oh, now that's a story in itself. You see, I'm a large animal vet. I had a practice back in Nashville… that's where I'm from… but hadn't set up my practice in Whiskey Ridge just yet…"

"How on Earth did you end up in Whiskey Ridge?"

"Well, now, which story do you want to hear?" she asked with a giggle.

Nash found himself smiling. This woman was actually nice. And she loved his father, evidently. A nice woman was in love with his father. Miracles apparently did happen.

"So here I am, my first day in town, when I run into Danny at the pet store…"

"Danny?" Nash said.

"Your father?" she responded laughing.

"Sorry. I don't think I've ever heard anyone refer to him by his real name. Everyone calls him Brick."

"Yeah, well I'm not everyone. And Brick makes him sound like he either has rocks in his head or he's a linebacker for the local football team."

"Sorry, I interrupted you…" Nash said, taking a handful of chips from a bowl on the kitchen island.

"Anyway, I saw Danny looking at some dog supplements. You know, for that old hound dog he keeps at the barn? Well, I knew he could order them online for half the price, but I sure didn't want the manager to hear me say that. No need to piss off my new fellow citizens, right?"

She was so easygoing as she spoke. Smiling and giggling to herself as she continued preparing what was sure to be the world's largest salad. And Nash, despite himself, couldn't help but smile with her. She was light. She had no pretense. She was just vivacious and elegant and funny. And he found himself feeling a little bit jealous of his father's good fortune to find such a woman so late in life.

"Well, we ended up chatting for so long in the aisle of the store that the place closed and asked us to leave. So we walked over to Duke's and had a nightcap. And we've basically been inseparable ever since!"

"Wow. That's great."

Lana looked up from her salad preparation and smiled at Nash.

"I know your father was a bit of a curmudgeon in his younger days, Nash. This isn't my first time at this rodeo, so to speak. But just because a person has made mistakes in the past doesn't mean they have to continue making them in the future. Give your Daddy a chance. I promise you won't be sorry if you just leave open the slightest possibility that he's a better man today than he was when you last spoke to him."

"Sounds like he owes that transformation to you," Nash said softly, being careful that his father wasn't back in the house yet.

"People don't change unless they really want to, my boy. And Lord knows, change is hard. Danny wanted to be a better man for you boys... and probably for me too a little bit," she said with a wink.

Before Nash could speak, he heard the back door open. Brick appeared behind him and then leaned over to kiss Lana on the cheek as she cut up onions and struggled not to cry.

"Goodness gracious, woman, how big of a salad are you making?" Billy said as he walked into the house with a plate stacked with steaks.

"It's just like Southern hairstyles. The bigger they are, the closer to God!"

Everyone laughed at that, and Nash had a momentary glimpse of what a normal, happy family felt like - something he'd never known in his whole life. And something he'd never realized - until just now - that he needed so much.

EMMY SAT NERVOUSLY in the chair. Her mother, on the other hand, sat beside her without a care in the world, reading some trashy magazine while smacking her chewing gum.

"Mother, could you please stop cracking that gum?"

"Could you please stop correcting me?" Pauline said without looking up. "Good Lord, would you look at her butt? That has to be fake. God don't make butts that shape..." She held out the magazine to Emmy.

"Stop it! Aren't you the slightest bit anxious to hear what Dr. Gaines has to say about your bloodwork?"

"Nah. I've had more blood drawn over my life than ten people combined. No big whoop," she said, looking back down at her magazine.

"Well, I wish I could be as anxiety free as you are."

"Emmy, you've never been anxiety free a day in your life. You came out of my loins all wound up tighter than a ball of yarn."

"Thanks a lot for that visual image, Mom."

"Hello, ladies," Dr. Gaines said as he walked into his office. "Sorry to keep you waiting."

"Doctors always keep you waiting, mainly because they're usually arrogant people in general," Pauline said flippantly before tossing her magazine on the side table.

"Mom!"

"It's okay, Emmy. Your Mom and I go way back," he said with a smile.

"Apologize," Emmy said under her breath.

"Apologize for what? The doc here knows I was just messing around. Right, Doc?"

"Of course," he said, shooting a grin at Emmy. "I have your blood test results."

"Am I pregnant?"

Emmy put her head in her hands. "Do you see what I'm dealing with here?"

"I understand, Emmy. And it's okay. Your mother has always had her own particular sense of humor. Anyway, Miss Pauline, you have one smart daughter here. She was totally right about your B12 levels. They are incredibly low. Have you been feeling tired lately?"

"I'm old, Doc. Of course I feel tired."

"What about pins and needles in your hands or feet? Any of that?"

"Sometimes."

"Well, what we're going to do today is start you on some B12 shots. You will come in regularly for shots and then we'll reassess in a few weeks to see what your levels are, okay?"

"Sounds like a plan," Pauline said before digging through her purse for another piece of gum. "Say, Doc, do you happen to have any gum?"

Dr. Gaines smiled. "Why don't you go talk to Kathleen at

78

the front desk. I think she has some treats we give the younger kids."

Pauline grabbed her purse and left the room in search of more gum.

"Sorry about her. She can be a bit…"

"It's okay, Emmy. Your mother has been seeing me for a good ten years. I know her personality well."

"So do you think these shots might help her forgetfulness?"

Dr. Gaines sighed and sat back against his brown leather chair. "Maybe. I've been doing some research, and I want to try a regimen that has helped others with dementia symptoms. But don't get your hopes up just in case it doesn't work out, okay?"

"Any hope is a good thing right now. I really appreciate you testing her."

As Emmy walked with Pauline to the car, she felt such a sense of gratitude for Nash. At least there was a possibility that her mother might get better, thus freeing her up to start her life over again.

The only problem was she didn't even know where to start.

NASH GROANED as Emmy worked his calf muscle. He'd only been in therapy for a couple of weeks now, but he was already seeing some progress.

He spent most of his day out of the wheelchair, but he was using a walker instead which made him feel a bit like he should be living at the retirement village. Maybe Pauline's room was still available.

"How's that pressure?" Emmy asked.

"It's fine."

"You okay?" Emmy asked.

"Yeah. Just wish I was progressing faster."

"I'm doing the best I can, Nash."

He tilted his head and looked at her. "It's not about what you're doing. It's about the fact that I'm apparently getting old and decrepit, so my body isn't bouncing back like I'd hoped."

"You have to give it time, Nash. We've talked about this. Turn over."

Nash gingerly turned over. He was getting faster at it, but certainly not back to normal.

Emmy stacked more pillows behind him, and he scooted up to face her.

"Lift this arm," she said as he started working on his range of motion exercises. Although she threw other things in each week, he had a specific set of basic exercises they always did.

"Listen, you're getting better every session. And if you're doing your home exercises too, I expect exponential progress each week."

"But when can I ride again?" Nash asked.

Emmy stopped for a moment. "There are no guarantees. We've talked about this. But…"

"But what?"

"I think you're winning the fight against the physical injuries you have, Nash."

"That's good, right?"

"Of course. But I'm not so sure you're dealing with the emotional stuff."

Nash rolled his eyes. "Don't get all woo woo on me, Emmy."

She laughed. "It's not woo woo. Emotional scars can have a great impact on the physical body. You may not heal fully until you deal with those things."

"Like what? How am I emotionally scarred?" he said,

holding his hand up to his heart and fluttering his eyelashes.

"You think it's funny, but it's real. You haven't dealt with the idea that you're getting older and that riding bulls may not be in the cards for you anymore. You haven't dealt with the emotions of being replaced by younger riders. You haven't dealt with the issues with your father. You haven't dealt our..." she stopped herself, her eyes widening for a moment as if she'd almost let something slip out.

Nash stared at her for a moment, not breaking eye contact. "I haven't dealt with losing the love of my life?"

She cleared her throat and looked down at his arm. "We don't discuss personal issues here, Nash. This is therapy. Remember our agreement?"

"Then let's go somewhere else."

～

"Where's your Mom?" Nash asked as they walked into her small house.

"My cousin Debbie took her out for a day of beauty," Emmy said as she opened the mini blinds and created a plume of dust. She coughed and fanned her hand across her face.

"And what does a day of beauty include?" Nash asked with a laugh as he lowered himself to the 70's styled sofa.

Emmy sat down in the arm chair next to him and smiled. "Well, let's see. Eyebrow waxing, a hair cut, upper lip waxing..."

Nash put up his hand. "Please stop. I shouldn't have asked."

"Want some coffee?"

"Nah. I'm good," he said. Emmy had to admit she was stalling. Never in a million years did she expect Nash to want to talk about their past. He'd never been an overly communicative sort, probably as a result of living with his hard headed, stubborn, jackwad of a father.

"So, what're we doing here, Nash?" she finally summoned the courage to ask.

"I think you may be right."

"Wow. You think I'm right about something? Has Dr. Miller upped your dosage?"

Nash chuckled. "I'll have you know I'm one-hundred percent off pain pills and muscle relaxants, thank you very much. Just taking a little ibuprofen here and there."

"I'm proud of you for that. I know how hard those medications can be to withdraw from."

"It was hard, but Dr. Miller helped me taper the dosages."

Now they were small talking. She knew this avoidance tactic very well.

"So I'll ask again... what am I right about?"

Nash sat back against the sofa and took in a deep breath.

"Look, I know that I haven't dealt with a lot of things in my past that I need to. I feel this weight on me all the time, and I know my blood pressure was up at my last appointment. So I think you may be right that it's hindering my progress."

"You're still doing really good, Nash. Better than I expected. Your range of motion is..."

"Em."

"What?"

"Let me talk."

"Sorry."

"I really like my Dad's fiancee. She's nice, and she has changed him, I think. He's softer. Kinder. More open to change."

"That's good, I guess." Emmy still had her own hard feelings against Brick, but she decided not to remind Nash of that right now.

"There's a lot I may need to talk out with someone... a professional, I guess."

"I know of a couple of great therapists at the hospital. Dr. Nance and Dr. Gable both come highly recommended..."

"Thanks. I'll look into both of them. But that's not why I wanted to talk to you alone, Em."

"Oh?"

"I think we both need to air out some things. Don't you?"

Emmy looked down at her hands. They'd never really talked about it once things ended so abruptly. There were no letters or phone calls. One day, it was just over. And there were plenty of feelings to go around. Abandonment. Sorrow. Confusion. Anger. Betrayal. So many emotions that it was hard to keep up with.

But did she really want to open that can of worms? She was just starting to get used to being around Nash again. She was able to do her job and be cordial without strangling him or kissing him.

"Do you really think it's a good idea that we go down that road, Nash? It's the past. Maybe it's better that we leave it there."

"I would've said the same thing a few weeks ago. But when you almost die, it changes your perspective. And I know I wouldn't feel right if I didn't say some things."

She swallowed hard and tried to ignore the fluttering heartbeat in her chest. This was a time of her life she hadn't visited in awhile.

"Okay."

Nash took another moment as if he was gathering his thoughts.

"I was young and stupid. I was scared when you told me you were pregnant, and I made the worst mistake of my life in the way I reacted."

Emmy stared into space, unable to make eye contact.

Finding out she was pregnant just before she turned eighteen years old hadn't been in her longterm plans. She was ready to leave for college at the time, but instead found herself peeing on a stick in the drugstore bathroom.

"I should've been more supportive, Em. I should have stopped the whole rodeo thing and told my Dad to back off."

Brick had gone ballistic when Nash told him Emmy was pregnant. He'd confronted Emmy himself one day when her mother wasn't home. Of course, Emmy was still basically a kid, and that had rattled her in a big way at the time.

Emmy still couldn't speak. She didn't know what to say. That it was okay? It wasn't. That she forgave him? She wasn't sure she did.

"Your Dad told me to get an abortion, Nash. Told me that I was going to ruin your life," she said softly.

"I know. I'm so sorry, Emmy. He was so wrong, and I believe it's why I still can't connect with him no matter how hard I try. I'm still angry about it all."

"And then the day it happened... the day I lost our baby... you weren't there. You had already taken off to Vegas. All I had was my mother to support me, and she isn't exactly the best person to help in times of crisis."

"God, Emmy, I'm sorry." He slid to the edge of the sofa and looked at her. "I've beat myself up a million times over not being there when you miscarried our baby. But you have to understand that I didn't know about the miscarriage until weeks later, and by then I was afraid you wouldn't take my calls..."

"You didn't even try, Nash. Not one letter or phone call. You just left me here to deal with all alone."

"I was an idiot at the time. And I was scared..."

Emmy stood up, her face feeling flush and tears threatening to spill over. "You don't think I was scared? I was terrified! My whole life was about to come to an end before it even started. I wasn't ready to be a mother, but I was committed to it. You left thinking I was pregnant, and you didn't have plans to come back and be a father!"

Nash tried to stand, but fell back to the couch without his walker to use for assistance. He sighed and rubbed his eyes.

"I did plan to come back. That's how I found out about the miscarriage."

"Why did you leave me like that then? You said you loved me."

"I loved you more than anyone in this world, Em. You weren't just some high school crush. Even then, I believed I'd spend the rest of my life with you. I just panicked."

"You panicked? Well, what do you think I was doing?"

"No, you don't understand. I wasn't panicked about having a baby with you. I was excited about that."

"Then why were you panicked?" she asked, sitting back down.

"Because I wanted to be able to provide for both of you. I wanted to buy you a ring... the kind you deserved. I wanted to buy everything our baby needed. And I knew my Dad would make my life, and yours, miserable if I worked for him. I was going to go to Vegas, make as much money as I could and be back before the baby was born with a big diamond ring in my hand. I knew if I told you why I was leaving that you'd say not to go, that we would make it work somehow. But I was a broke kid with no college education and no way to provide for you and the baby. So I took off thinking you'd understand once I got back, that you'd forgive me when you saw I was just trying to make money for us. But then my father called me and told me about the miscarriage. Apparently Pauline had confronted my Dad and told him off."

"So why didn't you call? Why didn't you come home then?"

"I was a coward. By then, I was already getting a name for myself in Vegas. I knew my Dad was angry at me for leaving his business. I knew you probably hated me. I just stayed away hoping you could go on with your life."

Emmy allowed a stray tear to run down her cheek. "I needed you," she whispered.

Nash reached across and tried to take her hand, but Emmy stood up.

"Please don't do that," she said, rubbing her hand on the front of her pants.

"I don't know how else to make amends, Em."

"Honestly, I'm not sure it's possible."

Nash cleared his throat. "Fair enough. But I hope maybe someday we can at least be friends."

Emmy didn't speak. "I have to get back to work."

"Of course."

Emmy retrieved his walker and slid it in front of him before asking if he needed a ride back home.

"Nah, it's only a few blocks and I need the exercise if I want to…"

"Get back to your real life?" she said, finishing his sentence.

"Yeah. I think that will be better for both of us."

"I'll see you Monday," Emmy said as she walked him to the door.

"Look, if you're not comfortable working with me, I can find…"

"No. As I told you before, I'm a professional. I don't quit on people."

A silence hung in the air as Nash seemed to get her double meaning. He walked out and down the sidewalk without looking back.

CHAPTER 9

*E*mmy spent the weekend thinking about Nash and all that he'd said. Could she ever forgive him? Did she even need to?

After all, they weren't dating, and they didn't need to be friends. He was her patient, simple as that. She wanted to believe that, but her heart wouldn't let her.

The reality was that when she looked at him, she saw her whole life and where it had gone off track all those years ago. She'd never imagined a future without Nash in it. If she was being honest with herself, she'd always had him in the back of her mind, even when she was married.

"I know there was something else we needed…" Emmy muttered to herself as she sat at the kitchen table with her grocery shopping list. "I have eggs, milk, ketchup…"

"We need fabric softener. But remember to get the kind with the little bear and not the kind with the big purple flower. That stuff smells like a whorehouse," Pauline said, never looking up from her crossword puzzle. For as long as Emmy could remember, her mother always spent Sunday evenings at the kitchen table with a cup of coffee and her beloved crossword puzzle.

"I know there was something else…"

"Toilet paper. But get the double ply kind. You've got to stop trying to save a buck. That last stuff you got was worse than truckstop bathroom toilet paper."

Emmy stopped writing and looked at her mother. How was she remembering this stuff? It dawned on her that the B12 shots must be working because her mother could never remember stuff like that.

"Mom, do you remember when my dental appointment is, by chance?"

Pauline chuckled as she filled in the blanks, a look of satisfaction on her face. "The third of next month. Maybe you need some of those shots, Em."

Emmy smiled to herself as she finished her list. Maybe things were looking up after all. If her mother was able to care for herself, she could go home to Atlanta sooner than she thought. Only Atlanta just didn't feel like home anymore.

"I HAVE to say I'm impressed, Nash. Your range of motion is really improving," Emmy said as she finished their exercises for the day. "Look how far you can lift that arm now."

Nash smiled half heartedly. "Yeah, it's definitely better."

"What's wrong now?"

"I just want to get back to normal life."

"Vegas?"

Nash chuckled. "Actually, no. I just want to be able to do normal things. Take a walk or a hike. Spend time in nature. Take a shower without holding onto something."

Emmy cocked her head and thought for a moment. "I can help with some of that."

Nash grinned. "Okay, please follow me over this way toward the shower," he said, playfully waving his hand sideways like a game show model.

"Ha ha, very funny. You have some time right now?"

"Well, I can fit you in between my conference call and meeting with my financial adviser."

Emmy stared at him for a moment before realizing he was joking.

"Right. Okay. Come on. I want to take you somewhere."

Nash was maneuvering his walker so well that sometimes he could get by with just a cane. They loaded his walker into her car, just in case, but when they arrived a few miles away at their destination, he only brought his cane with him.

"Where are we going?" he asked as they got out at a nondescript parking lot and headed toward a wooded path.

"You don't know where you are?" Emmy asked, a surprised look on her face.

"Well, I haven't been to Whiskey Ridge in years, and this parking lot wasn't here when I left."

"I've been gone a long time too, but I can't believe you'd ever forget this place..." She smiled before turning and heading toward the path.

Nash followed slowly behind her, but they weren't very far into the path before he tripped on a small root and bumped into her back.

"Oh, man... Sorry," he said, holding onto her for dear life as she leaned over and retrieved his cane from the ground. "Maybe this isn't a good idea."

Emmy looked up at him. "You can do this. I should've supported you better. Sorry I walked ahead of you. Here, hold onto this arm." She held her upper arm out toward him, and he slowly took hold of it for more support. "It's not a long walk, I promise."

They walked along together, mostly quiet, with Nash concentrating on where he was walking.

"Look at that," she whispered as a deer crossed the path about twenty feet in front of them. It stared at them for a moment before slowly walking into the woods. "I forgot how peaceful this place could be."

"Yeah, well to be fair, we were kids back then. We weren't exactly looking for peace, were we?"

She laughed. "I guess you're right. We were looking for adventure. Remember when we all jumped off Cherokee Cliff? That lake was freezing!"

"If I remember correctly, you tried to do a flip and did a belly flop instead," Nash said with a laugh.

"That hurt for a week! I didn't have as much padding around my midsection as I do now."

Nash cut his eyes over at her and smiled, his dimples on full display. "Well, Doc, I don't see anything wrong with your figure."

"Nash…" she chided.

"Hey, I might have a bum arm and leg, but I can still appreciate beauty when I see it."

"Yes, and this forest *is* beautiful," she said, staring straight ahead and trying to change the subject.

"You know, I remember the day I first saw you. You were standing outside that ring, and I was so distracted I'm surprised I didn't get hurt that day too."

Emmy stopped and looked at him. "I don't know if it's a good idea to walk down memory lane, Nash."

He sighed. "Why wouldn't it be a good idea to remember good things?"

Emmy turned and started walking again. "Fine. But only good things. No potentially upsetting or anger producing topics."

"Yes, ma'am," he said with a smile. Gosh, his smiles were

deadly. He'd gotten away with everything as a teenage boy simply because of that smile. And that thick, wavy head of hair. And those broad shoulders and muscular arms…

"Remember when we TP'd the school senior year?"

"Um, that was you and the McAllister boys. I was at home being a good girl!"

"Yeah, right. When we met up in my truck that night, you were certainly not being a good girl. I remember getting in all kinds of hot water over that hicky you put on my neck!"

Emmy had to laugh. Those were the good days. When there were no bills, no ex husbands, no life altering decisions.

Truth be told, she remembered the day she met Nash like it was yesterday. Watching him work with the horses and bulls gave her feelings that she didn't even understand at the time.

He'd been hot as a teenager, but even as a somewhat maimed grown man, he was even hotter now. His jawline was more square and grown up. His hair seemed thicker, but with flecks of silver starting to peek through here and there. His eyes seemed more tired, though, and that made her sad. Sometimes life takes its toll.

"Oh wow. I think I know where you're taking me. The question is, why?"

Emmy simply smiled and kept walking. The woods were her happy place. Even as a kid, she'd loved sneaking away to read under the shade of one of the massive oak trees that dotted the mountains around her hometown. Until now, she hadn't realized how much she'd missed the landscape. There were no honking car horns or massive glass-faced buildings. Instead, she could only hear the crunching of the leaves beneath their feet and the occasional bird tweeting.

"Follow me," she said as they turned down a path to the right. "Be careful of these tree roots."

Nash looked down as the descended the pathway, tripping a bit as he diverted his attention. Emmy grabbed his good arm before he could do much damage.

"Thanks," he said softly. They froze for a moment, looking at each other, before Emmy let go and turned back toward the path.

"Can you hear that?" she asked, a smile spreading across her face.

Nash smiled too, recognizing where they were headed. "I knew it."

They walked down the path a bit further and came to a clearing where there was nothing but a mixture of jagged and smooth rocks, steep cliffs and raging water with side pools of completely calm water.

"I can't believe you brought me back to this place," Nash said as he looked side to side, taking in all of the scenery. His face showed what was going on inside his head; memories were raging past just like the water in front of him.

"Come on," Emmy said, reaching out her hand to help him onto a large rock that sat next to the water. He took her hand and their eyes met for a long moment until Emmy broke their gaze and pulled him along with her.

For a moment, she was back in high school. She'd held his hand many times walking to this same rock. In fact, many things had happened near these waters all those years ago.

Nash struggled up onto the rock and sat down. He was out of breath which was hard for Emmy to see. His injuries had really taken a toll on him.

"It's been forever since I came out here," Emmy said as they sat there looking at the water move past them.

"Me too," Nash said before he started laughing.

"What?"

"I remember this one time, me and Billy came out here because he was convinced he could jump from that rock over there to this one. I knew he couldn't do it, especially without falling on his ass. But he bet me ten bucks, and I hadn't gotten my allowance that week because my Dad said I didn't cut the grass the right way."

"Ugh. Your father is…"

"Em. Let's not go there."

"Right."

"Anyway, Billy gets up on that rock and pounds his chest like Tarzan before taking this running leap. A group of our buddies and their girlfriends were out here too. I think you were working or something. Anyway, he runs but slips at the end of the rock and slides down the face of it. What he didn't count on was this jagged piece on the face of the rock that caught the edge of his swim trunks. When he finally got loose, he was naked as a jaybird holding onto the side of that rock for dear life while we all laughed and made fun of any body parts we saw."

Emmy laughed hard. She could just imagine Billy doing a thing like that, and it brought back fond memories of better times.

"Billy was a nut back then," she said.

"Billy is still a nut."

"Do you think he'll ever settle down?"

"I don't know. I doubt it. He seems to love single life. Now me, I never enjoyed single life. I wanted to be tied down."

Emmy giggled. "You said tied down."

Nash cut her a glance and smiled. "I remember when we tried that…"

"Nash Collier!" she said, smacking him on the arm. "And you know that isn't true anyway."

"It was a fun thought," he said under his breath. "So why did you bring me here, Emmy?"

"Because you need to get out of the therapy room and into the world again."

"I know that, but why here? Why specifically this place?"

"No real reason. I just remembered this place."

"Come on, Em."

"Don't read anything into it, Nash. It's just a place," she said, their eyes meeting for a brief moment before she continued. "Besides, my job is to get you back to Vegas as soon as possible, right? And maybe your dream woman is waiting there for you right now."

God, she hoped he didn't look at her face right now or it was going to give her away for sure.

~

OF COURSE, she knew what this place had meant to both of them. There was no way she'd forgotten, Nash thought to himself. This place had been "their place". Many firsts were experienced here. First time they held hands. First picnic. First kiss. Even their first slow dance using a boom box he'd found in his brother's room.

And another first that a person didn't discuss in public.

And she'd brought him here. Out of all the places in Whiskey Ridge they could've gone for a therapy field trip, she'd chosen this place. Nash couldn't help but read more into it.

And he had no idea how he felt about it all. For weeks, all he could think about was getting back to Vegas. Getting back into the rodeo game. Now, all he could think about was a boy and a girl sitting on this same rock all those years ago.

"My Mom is doing so much better," Emmy suddenly said.

"What?"

"My Mom. The shots are helping her memory. She remembered most of our grocery list when I couldn't!"

"Maybe you need some shots," Nash said, nudging her arm with his elbow.

"Stress does that to me, I guess."

"Have you heard from your husband?"

"Ex husband now. And no. He left me in the lurch, but I'm working things out."

"I'm sure you are, but if you ever want to talk about it..."

"Thanks," she said, looking over at him. "You always were my best friend, Nash Collier."

That made him feel both good and bad, and he wasn't sure why.

"So do you own a home in Atlanta?"

"No. We were renting an apartment in a high rise near the restaurant."

"So that's where you'll go back to?" he asked, trying to sound nonchalant, but really wondering what her plans were.

"No. I lost it."

"Oh. Sorry. Well, I'm sure you'll find someplace else. You always land on your feet." He hated the way that sounded, as if her problems weren't real.

"I've always been forced to land on my feet. It doesn't mean I like it, Nash. But when the only person you can count on is yourself..."

"I'm sorry."

"No, I didn't mean that like it sounded. I'm sorry."

They both smiled sadly at each other and then stared back at the water.

"Her name was Kaylee," she said softly.

"Whose name was Kaylee?"

"Our daughter," she said, a tear welling in her eye. "She was so tiny, Nash."

He reached over and took her hand, and she let him.

"Oh, Emmy... I'm so sorry I wasn't there..."

She squeezed his hand and smiled sadly. "I forgive you."

"How could you forgive me? I don't even forgive myself,"

he said, struggling with tears of his own. "That was my baby girl, and I ran out on both of you."

Emmy turned and wiped away the stray tear that escaped from his eye. "We were just kids, and we had a lot of pressure. I understand it better now. I didn't realize how hurt I was about it all these years... until I saw you again. I'm sorry I got so angry at you, but I think I needed that release."

"How far along were you?"

"Honestly, I don't know. I just remember that day. I started having a lot of pain, so my mother took me to the ER. There were a lot of people rushing around... and then it was over. My Mom made them bring Kaylee to me. I think she just knew that I would regret never seeing her. She was so tiny, Nash. She fit in the palm of my hand."

He sat there listening to her, wishing things could've been different all those years ago. Emmy had been the woman of his dreams, the only person in the world who ever truly understood him. To lose her the way that he did had shaken him to the core.

"Who did she look like?" Nash asked.

Emmy smiled. "Well, she was still so tiny it was hard to tell, but I swear she was going to have your nose."

Nash reached up and touched his nose. "Yikes."

Emmy laughed as she wiped the tears from her face. She smacked him on the arm. "Stop it! You have a great nose."

"You know, I'm glad you told me all this. It was hard to hear, but I've wondered for years if you knew if it was a boy or girl. Now I can know that we had a baby girl, and her name was Kaylee."

Emmy smiled. "We have a little grave marker for her at the church cemetery... if you'd ever like to go visit her."

"I would like that a lot. Thank you for telling me."

"We didn't put our last name on the marker. I think my

Mom was a little embarrassed by it all at the time, but she never said so."

"Things were different back then, I guess," Nash said simply.

Emmy stared at her feet, dangling a few inches above the water. "And don't think I've forgotten all of our memories from this place, Nash."

He cleared his throat. "So you do remember?"

"Of course. This was our place, and it always will be. You know, back then I was certain that one day we'd get married right here. Just something small with our family and friends."

Nash swallowed hard. "You thought we'd get married one day?"

"Of course. You didn't?" she asked with a laugh.

"I wasn't sure. My parents didn't exactly show me a glowing example of marriage."

"True. Are you still liking his new fiancee?"

"She's great. I can't believe I'm saying that, but she's changed him for the better."

"Well, I'm glad. For your sake. And best of luck to her because she'll need it."

It was obvious Emmy still held a lot of resentment toward Brick.

"We'd better head back. I've got an appointment after lunch, so I need to eat a bite."

"Right. Listen, thanks for bringing me here, Em. It was nice."

"You're doing good, Nash. Don't worry. You'll be back to Vegas in no time, and this will all be a memory again." She smiled, although it looked forced, and waved her hand around the river.

The only problem was, he wasn't sure he wanted it to just be a memory anymore.

CHAPTER 10

*H*e'd texted her early in the morning asking her to meet him near their favorite spot by the river. As she walked down the path, quiet in the early hours of the day, she felt her stomach doing flip flops. She hadn't felt this way since their first date all those years ago.

The morning sun was peeking down between the trees, lighting up the pine straw on the pathway, making it look like little strands of gold in front of her.

And there he was, sitting on the split rail fence, the rays of sun lighting him up front behind like some kind of Southern cowboy angel. His hair, still so wavy and thick, looked speckled with flecks of gold.

He said nothing. He just smiled that dimpled smile and waved her over. His cane was nowhere to be seen, and he was wearing those rugged cowboy boots and dusty blue jeans she'd always loved so much.

She walked toward him, and he swiftly pulled her up beside him, staring into her eyes without saying a word. Just as she was about to ask him why he'd called her there, he slipped his right hand into her hair, pulling her lips to his. It felt so familiar, so warm, so welcoming. His tongue slowly made its way between her parted lips, ever so gently touching hers...

"Emmy! Wake up!"

Emmy slowly opened her eyes, begging God and any other entities in the Universe to let her see a handsome face. Instead, it was her mother standing over her in the living room where she'd apparently fallen asleep after work.

"Jeez, do you have to yell so loudly, Mother?" She sat up and rubbed her eyes. "And turn down that TV! We need to get your hearing checked."

"I turned it up to try to wake you up, but nothing was working. Good Lord, I almost called the paramedics." Pauline sat down next to her and grinned.

"What?"

"So who was he?"

"Who was who?"

"The man in your dream."

Emmy's eyes opened wider as she stared at her mother. How had those shots given her magical powers to see inside of Emmy's dreams?

"I don't know what you're talking about," Emmy said as she stood up and walked to the kitchen.

"Uh huh, sure. Then why were you smiling so big?"

"If I was smiling so big, then why on Earth did you wake me up from what was obviously a good dream?" Emmy asked as she poured herself a much-needed cup of coffee.

Pauline laughed. "It was Nash, wasn't it?"

"Why would you say that?"

"Well, because you just blushed when I mentioned his name. And because Hester Jenkins saw you two going to the river the other day. And we all know what goes on down at the river..."

"Mother! Nothing of the sort is going on between me and Nash. It was simply a field trip to help with his rehab."

Pauline crossed her arms and stared at her daughter. "You deserve more than this, Emmy."

Emmy looked at her mother, and for the first time in years, she felt a motherly presence from her. She'd gotten used to being in the parent role, but it was nice to hear her talk this way.

"What do you mean?"

"I mean that Nash is your soul mate, and he made some big mistakes back then. But marrying that idiot, Steve, was a big mistake you made. Now you both have a second chance."

"No, we don't. Nash wants to go back to his Vegas life. And I have a life in Atlanta."

"No you don't, Emmy. You and I both know that. I'm not so old that I can't see what's happening right in front of me. You love Whiskey Ridge, and you only left because of the memories all those years ago. Now that you're back, you smile more. You laugh more. You love your job, don't you?"

Emmy sighed. "Yes, I do love it. But... and please don't take offense to this... I'd consider my life a failure if I came home to Whiskey Ridge and lived with my mother at my age."

Pauline chuckled. "Well, honey... and don't take offense to this... I don't want to live with you either."

"Mom!"

"Well, I don't. Look, Emmy, we're very different. I can't stand not having my collections in my house, and I might want to entertain..."

"Gross."

"Hey, I'm not dead yet, and it might interest you to know that a few suitors are interested in me."

"Please stop talking," Emmy said, putting her head in her

hands. She couldn't help but smile to herself. Her mother really was a firecracker.

"It's time for you to start over, Emmy. I don't need you hovering over me anymore. These shots are helping, and if you stay in Whiskey Ridge, you can check in on me from time to time. Just call first."

"Good Lord."

Pauline giggled and reached across the breakfast bar for her daughter's hand. "You're young. Don't waste time fretting over the past. Embrace the present."

"Have you been watching self improvement videos again?"

"Maybe, but that's neither here nor there. Listen, I've got plans tonight so I'm heading out for the evening."

"Plans?" Emmy asked as she followed her mother to the front door.

"Edgar Winston invited me to bingo at the VFW. Don't wait up," she said with a grin as she walked out the front door with one of her big gaudy purses slung over her shoulder.

Emmy decided then and there that her mother was right. She had to start living again. The question was where she would live and who would be in her life.

"PULL AS HARD AS YOU CAN," Emmy said as Nash tugged on the pulley. Getting him on the weight machines had helped a lot in the last couple of weeks. He was getting his strength back much quicker than anticipated and now rarely needed his cane unless they were walking long distances.

Nash let go of the pulley and wiped his brow as the metal clanged against the machine. "Dang, that one almost killed me! What are you trying to do to me?"

Emmy smiled. "Well, you see, it's my dream to slowly kill you by increasing the weight at each visit until the machine topples over on top of you." She did her best evil laugh and threw her head back.

"It feels like it!" Nash said as he slouched onto the padded massage table behind him. "My bicep really is hurting." He rubbed the muscle and winced.

"Here, let me take a look," Emmy said, rubbing her hand over his arm. She pushed into the knotted muscle as Nash jumped a little. "Right there?"

"Yeah. Man, that's tender."

"It will be for awhile. We're getting toward the end of treatment, and I'm really working your muscles."

Nash looked up at her. "We're near the end?"

Emmy smiled and looked at him. "Yes. You've done good, Nash. You'll be heading back to Vegas before you know it."

"Well, that sure is good news!" a voice boomed from the waiting area. Nash turned around and was shocked to see his buddy, Deke, standing there with a huge grin on his face.

"Deke?" he said, standing up. He couldn't believe his friend was standing there after not seeing him for weeks.

"In the flesh! Dang, brother, you've lost some weight. I thought Southern food was supposed to fatten you up!" Deke walked over and pulled his friend into a tight hug.

"Well, my therapist here tends to work me out so hard that I can't gain any weight."

Deke looked at Emmy and smiled. "They sure make pretty therapists up here in the mountains."

"Slow down, man. Sorry, Emmy. He doesn't see beautiful women very often. Mostly horses and bulls, if you get my drift."

Deke let out a loud laugh, so much so that other patients turned around.

"Why don't we take this visit outside to the courtyard?"

Emmy suggested, following them as they made their way to the small area outside the hospital's cafeteria.

"So, how's the circuit going?" Nash asked as they sat down on the concrete bench outside.

"Well, we're up a few points toward championships right now. Dylan Reynolds scooped first last weekend, and we got this weekend off so I thought I'd head across the country to see how my brother from another mother was doing."

"You've heard of these things called phones, right?" Nash asked.

"Yeah, but I've been busy lately. Plus, ain't it better to see my handsome face in person?"

Nash rolled his eyes. "He's over confident considering he couldn't beat me in competition for the last three years." Emmy smiled.

"Mr. Collier? We have some updated insurance papers we need to get signed," the hospital billing coordinator called from the doorway.

"Deke, behave. You okay out here with this guy?"

"I'm sure I'll be fine, Nash," Emmy said with a laugh.

DEKE WAS CERTAINLY A CHARACTER, and Emmy could see how he and Nash had become such good friends.

"So how's he really doing?" Deke finally asked after they sat there quietly for a few moments.

"I can't really talk about too much because of patient privacy laws…"

"Yeah yeah yeah. But is he coming home soon?"

Home. It was one of the first times it had dawned on Emmy that Nash thought of Vegas as home.

"I think so. He has far exceeded my expectations given how he came in initially."

"I know he's itching to get back to competition."

"I guess so."

"So, are ya'll... dating?"

Emmy blushed and giggled like a schoolgirl. "No. Not at all. He's my patient."

"Good. Then does that mean I can ask you to dinner?"

Emmy's breath caught in her throat for a moment.

"No, it does not. Jeez, Deke. You just met her!" Nash said from behind Emmy. She'd never been so happy to hear his voice.

"Can't blame a guy for trying," Deke said with a sly smile.

"Wrong woman," Nash said under his breath as he stepped between them. There was a warning tone in his voice that Emmy hadn't expected to hear, and she didn't know what to make of it.

"So, what's on the calendar for tonight?" Deke asked, rubbing his hands together.

"What do you mean?" Nash asked with a laugh.

"Well, I'm only here for a couple of days. Aren't you going to treat me to the grand tour of Whiskey Ridge? Aren't you going to wine and dine me?"

Nash rolled his eyes in Emmy's direction. "As for the grand tour, you probably saw most of the town as you were driving over here. But I think we can at least provide food to such a weary traveler."

Deke grinned. "Good! What's on the menu? Filet mignon?"

"How about ribs and a beer?"

"Even better!" Deke slapped Nash on the back, which made Emmy cringe a bit.

"Hey, careful with my patient," she said, reaching out instinctively and rubbing Nash's shoulder. He stilled for a moment and looked at her.

"Sorry. I didn't know he was such a dainty flower," Deke

said, interrupting the moment. Emmy removed her hand from Nash's shoulder.

"Well, you guys have fun." She turned and started walking toward the therapy offices.

"Um, excuse me? I meant both of ya'll," Deke called.

"Her?" Nash said.

"Me?" Emmy said at the same time.

"Listen, I've spent a lot of time with this idiot. We lived together for years. I need someone else there as a buffer to our boring and dull conversations about bulls and horses."

Nash laughed and nodded. "He makes a good point. Why don't we take him to The Wing Shack over by the river?"

Emmy stared at Nash for a moment. "Okay. Sure. Let me grab my purse and I'll meet you around front."

～

"So, he takes this horse by the reins and the thing bucks so hard that Nash goes flying up in the air and pops his shoulder out of the socket. But dang if he didn't pop the thing back in and still catch the freaking horse a few seconds later!"

Emmy cringed again. "Ouch. You popped your shoulder out?"

"I've done that a million times, Em. I ride bulls, remember?"

Nash winked at her, and she felt things that she shouldn't. But the romance didn't have time to register because she looked over to see Deke covered in barbecue sauce with a huge smile on his face.

"Man, these are good! I haven't been able to find the perfect wings in Vegas."

"And he's looked. Believe me. A lot. And I've had to hear

about it," Nash said, rolling his eyes as Deke tossed a wadded up napkin at him.

"I think these are winning the contest," Deke said as he licked the last bone clean. "Okay, so I have a question for you two."

"What?" Nash asked, polishing off the last bits of ice in the bottom of his glass of sweet tea.

"What's going on here exactly?"

"What's that supposed to mean?" Emmy asked as she continued working on her too-large pile of fries.

"The looks. The glances. The tension in the air when I asked you out."

"Maybe I just don't want you asking my physical therapist out."

"What about your dentist? Or is it all of your providers? Is your hairdresser off limits?"

"You're a funny guy," Nash groaned.

"Look, I just want to know."

"Maybe it's none of your damn business, Deke." Nash was getting irritated.

"It's okay, Nash. Let's just tell him." Emmy put on a serious face and looked at Deke. "Nash and I have joined a gang. We killed a very rich man and buried his money in the old box canyon. But now we'll have to kill you too. Nash, do you still have the pick ax?"

Nash burst out laughing as Deke sat back in his chair and pursed his lips. "Very funny. Now I'm even more convinced."

"Convinced of what?" Nash asked after he caught his breath.

"That you have feelings for this lady."

Silence hung in the air. Deke smiled with satisfaction.

"We were high school sweethearts," Nash said matter of factly.

"And now?"

"I'm his physical therapist. That's how small towns work."

"I'm still sensing something here..."

"You're like the rodeo version of Dr. Phil," Emmy said.

"Hey, I've got a lot more hair!"

"I wouldn't say a lot..." Nash said.

"Fine. I won't keep asking, but you're different, man."

"Different how?"

"You just seem more... relaxed. At peace."

"Maybe it's the mountain air," Nash said.

Emmy had to wonder if it was the mountain air or if Nash might still have feelings for her after all.

CHAPTER 11

"Make sure to ice that shoulder for twenty minutes as soon as you get home, Ms. Elbert," Emmy called to her last patient of the day. She'd already sent her assistant, Hillary, home for the day, and she was looking forward to a nice, hot bath once she got home.

"Excuse me, ma'am, I need a rub down please."

She turned to see Deke standing in the waiting room, a big goofy grin on his face.

"I'm sorry, but we don't offer 'rub downs,'" she said, using air quotes. "I think you're looking for a whorehouse."

Deke laughed. His laugh filled the entire room.

"Seriously, I just wanted to come and say goodbye. I'm heading back to Vegas tonight, so I'm driving to the airport today."

Emmy wiped down her last table and tossed the cloth into the laundry hamper nearby. "Well, I'll miss you and your witty repartee."

"I know you will. Listen, I was wondering if I could talk to you?"

Emmy was hesitant, but too curious to say no. "Sure."

"Can I sit?"

Emmy nodded her head as Deke sat on the edge of the massage table.

"Nash is my best friend."

"Yes, I gathered that."

"I only want the best for him. You know that, right?"

"Of course."

"I think he loves you."

Emmy's lungs felt like they emptied and wouldn't refill themselves.

"What?"

"Look, I've known Nash for many years. I've never seen him like this."

"Like what?"

Deke sighed. "Do you know that the whole time I've been here, Nash never asked me much of anything about the rodeo?"

Emmy was surprised by that. "He didn't?"

"Nope. And this is a guy who lived and breathed rodeo a few weeks ago."

"So what did he talk about then?"

"Family. Therapy. You, mainly."

"He did?"

"He talked about things you did when ya'll were growing up, your mother's memory issues, stuff like that. I know more about you than I do about him, Emmy."

"Okay. Well, I'm sorry he didn't talk about rodeo. Maybe he doesn't want to be reminded of what he's missed out on these last few weeks."

"No, you're misunderstanding me. I think it's great."

"You do?"

"Yes. Nash has always needed someone to ground him. He was over-focused on the rodeo. I kept telling him that we're getting older, and it might be time to settle into a real life, but he would always fight me on it. Now I know why."

"And why is that?" Emmy asked, confused.

"Oh, you silly woman. He never settled down because he had already met his soul mate a long time ago. No one else was ever going to be good enough, so he settled for bulls and horses."

"I don't think…" Emmy stammered.

"It's okay, Emmy. You'll realize I'm right soon enough," Deke said as he started toward the door.

"Deke, why are you telling me this anyway?"

He smiled as he opened the door. "Because I like you, and Nash deserves more in his life. Goodbye, Emmy."

And with that, Deke walked out, leaving Emmy with more questions than answers and a huge knot in her stomach.

"So, what are you doing for the 4th of July?" Nash asked as he stretched his arms out wide. Emmy had him using these stretchy bands that seemed to come straight from Satan himself.

"Ah, let me think. I'm working and then I will spend the evening at home eating ice cream and watching fireworks out the living room window."

"That sounds… dull. And where will Pauline be?"

"Actually, Mom has a date."

"A date?"

"Yep," she said, handing him a harder band. Nash sighed and took it, knowing that arguing was pointless. "Some guy she met at the VFW."

"Good old Pauline."

"Of course, we probably won't be living together by then anyway."

"What? Why?"

"We talked, and I'm getting my own place."

Nash stopped for a moment. "Back in Atlanta?"

"No, of course not. Atlanta is in the past for me, I think."

"Really? I thought you wanted to go back."

"There's nothing there for me anymore. Besides, I love my job here."

"Wow. So you're staying in Whiskey Ridge?"

"I suppose so. At least for the time being. Mom still needs me around, whether she'll admit it or not."

Nash smiled. "I'm happy for you, Em. You found your place, and it turned out to be right here at home."

"Home? I thought you considered Vegas to be your home?"

Nash cleared his throat. "I do. I meant this is your home."

"Oh. Right. Okay, let's switch to legs."

"So have you found a place?"

"I'm actually going to look at one after we finish. The man lives out of town and has a cottage up near the river that he wants to rent. It's a great deal, but he's only here for today so I have to go on my lunch break."

"Want some company?"

Nash was surprised to hear himself ask that. But for some reason, he really wanted to protect her, and meeting some random guy in the woods near the river just seemed too dangerous.

"If you want to come along, you're welcome to."

"Okay. Sounds like a plan." There was no way he was telling her he wanted to protect her because Emmy wouldn't take too kindly to him hovering over her. She was definitely an independent woman.

"So, how are things with your Dad and his love?"

"Great. She's really amazing. I can't wait for you to meet her."

"What?"

Nash stopped stretching the cord and it his lip.

"I mean… I don't actually know what that meant, to be honest. I just thought you'd like her."

Emmy smiled. "Well, I hope I do get to meet her some day."

"How about Wednesday evening?"

"The fourth of July?"

"Yeah. We're having a get together at the house."

"Your Dad's house?"

"Yes…"

"No…"

"Come on, Em. Give him a chance to…"

"To what, Nash? Yell at me? Make me feel small and worthless? Yeah, I've been on that ride before and it made me throw up," she said, turning and looking down at her chart.

"He's different now, Em. I don't know how to explain it."

Emmy looked at him and smiled sadly. "I'm happy for you, Nash. I think it's great that you're repairing your relationship with your father. I really do. But I don't have to subject myself to him and the memories… I'm sorry."

Nash nodded and sighed. "I understand."

"Are you ready to go see the cottage? He's meeting me there in fifteen minutes."

"Sure. Let's head out."

~

"MR. CRONIN, THIS PLACE IS WONDERFUL!" Emmy said to the older man as they walked out onto the back deck overlooking the river.

"So you'll take it?"

"Yes, absolutely. I brought the security deposit and first month's rent with me, so if you want to go ahead and sign the lease, I'd love to move in over the next few days if that works?"

"That would be wonderful. My wife and I will be traveling out West in our RV for the next few months, so having a reliable tenant in our house will be such a blessing."

Emmy read the lease and signed it before he gave her the keys and then headed out. Nash kept quiet for the most part, letting her take the lead.

When Mr. Cronin pulled away in his compact car, Emmy started jumping up and down.

"Can you believe I get to live here?"

Nash smiled. "Is someone a little excited?"

"This is my dream home, Nash. The big deck overlooking the river. The quiet. The garden area. I can plant tomatoes this year!"

"I hate tomatoes."

"Yeah, I remember. But I get to live here! How amazing is that?"

For the first time in months - actually, years - Emmy felt positive and hopeful about the future. She actually felt excited, which was almost a foreign feeling to her. The last time she'd truly felt excited was when she was a teenager and Nash had asked her out on a date for the first time. That thought caused butterflies in her stomach for a moment.

"This place really is great, Em. I'm so happy for you," he said, leaning over the railing and looking down at the moving water below. "Maybe I can get my life back on course soon too."

Emmy put her hand on his shoulder. "You're getting there, Nash. All of this will be a memory soon, don't worry."

Nash slowly turned and looked at her. "What if I don't want this to be a memory?"

"What?" Emmy's breath caught in her throat.

Nash took both of her hands. "Being with you these last few weeks has made me see that I've been running from memories for all these years, and maybe they weren't as scary as I thought."

Emmy smiled. "Some of them were."

"Thank you for not hating me, Emmy."

She couldn't help herself as she hugged him tightly, taking in the scent of his cologne. "I could never hate you, Nash. You were the great love of my life."

Dang. Why had she said that? Freaking cologne.

Nash pulled back and looked at her. "You still are the great love of my life, Emmy." Before she could respond or think of any rational thought, he slid his hand up the side of her face and leaned in, pressing his lips softly to hers.

Emmy froze in place, closing her eyes as she took in the moment. It had been so many years since she'd felt his lips against hers, smelled the faint aroma of strong coffee on his breath.

And then he was gone. He pulled back and took a deep breath.

"I'm sorry, Em." He turned and looked at the river once more. "Too many memories. It almost feels like no time has passed."

"But it has," Emmy said softly. Truthfully, she wanted another kiss more than she wanted her next breath, but she wasn't about to admit it to him.

"Yes, it has. And, no pun intended, a lot of water under the bridge."

"I think a pun was intended," she said with a sad chuckle. "I wish things could've been different."

Nash turned to her again, a sadness in his eyes. "Me too. But we're in a good place now, right?"

"We are."

"Good. I don't want to lose that. I've missed having you in my life all these years. More than I knew, I think."

Emmy touched his arm. "I've missed you too."

"And we both know that starting something up wouldn't be…"

"Right. Of course. You're going across the country, and this is good. This relationship we have now is… good."

Nash smiled. "Seeing you smile again makes me happy."

Emmy looked out over the river. "I finally feel hopeful again. You know, like there might be a real life out there for me. For so long, I thought I needed Steve to take care of me, but now I realize that I can take care of myself. I feel peaceful here in Whiskey Ridge, and I didn't think that was possible. That cloud of darkness that I used to feel when I came back here is gone, and now it feels like home again."

"You belong here, Em. You always have. And the next man you fall in love with dang well better take care of you or he'll have me to deal with."

Emmy smiled, but her heart ached at the same time. The next man she fell in love with? That didn't seem possible.

"So, since you're in a celebratory mood, will you please reconsider my dinner invitation?" Nash crinkled his eyes and put his hands together in a praying position.

"Why is this so important to you?" she asked.

"I don't know. I guess because I need some closure?"

"And how would this be closure exactly?" she asked, leaning against the deck railing.

Nash laughed. "I don't really know, to be honest. I just know I want you there, Em. Please?"

She took a deep breath and smiled. "Fine. But only because I want to brag about my new house and see who this patient woman is who has decided to hitch her star to your father's wagon."

115

~

"So he kissed you?" Debbie said, her eyes wide as she sat across from Emmy on the expansive deck. The river was roaring today, making conversation a little more difficult than normal.

"Yes, but it was over very quickly, trust me. He pulled back like I was a live power line."

"Did he say why?"

"Sort of. He doesn't want to lose our friendship, he likes where we are, blah blah blah." Emmy sipped her coffee and looked at her cousin.

"And how do you feel about that?"

"Well, I told him…"

"That's not what I asked. I asked how you *feel*."

Emmy smiled at Debbie. "I have no idea."

"I think you do."

"It doesn't matter, Deb. He's almost well enough to go back to Vegas. He has a life there. And he sure isn't going to give all that up for Whiskey Ridge."

"No. But I bet he'd give it all up for another chance with you."

Emmy sighed. "I don't want him to."

"What do you mean you don't want him to?"

"I want Nash to be happy, and if Vegas is where he's happy, then that's what I want for him. If being with me is going to make him miserable because it would require him to come back to Whiskey Ridge, then I don't want that for him."

"Em…"

"Debbie, please stop. Nash and I are destined to be just friends and that's all. And that's okay."

Debbie smiled at her sadly. "I think you want to believe that, my sweet cousin, but I sure don't think it's the truth."

CHAPTER 12

*N*ash drove up the driveway to Emmy's new rental house. It was so perfectly her with its big front porch with the log swing sitting at one end. It felt like home. *She* felt like home.

"Stop it, man. You can't do this," Nash muttered to himself as he shut off the car. "Your life is in Vegas. There's no sense in dredging up the past." This was the mantra he'd been repeating to himself for days, especially after his hasty stolen kiss.

Kissing her, even as chastely as he did, had brought back a rush of memories and feelings he thought he'd left way back in the past. But now, every time she touched him at therapy or even looked at him across the room, his stomach flip flopped and his palms would sweat. And yet she seemed unaffected.

"She doesn't feel that way about you, so just be cool," he said to himself. He was talking to himself a lot lately which was making him a bit worried about his sanity.

He walked up the front steps and rang the doorbell. Inviting her to his family's cookout had been a spur of the moment idea, but begging her to reconsider her initial "no" had been surprising even to him.

Emmy opened the door, and he literally felt his breath leave him. God, she was a gorgeous creature, and the years had only made her more beautiful.

There was a wisdom in her eyes now. The pain he'd seen in those first few weeks had vanished, and her smile was present more often now. He liked to think he had something to do with that.

"Wow. You look... great," Nash said, stammering like an idiot. She was wearing a red sundress that perfectly showed off her freckled shoulders. He's always loved those freckles that dotted her skin during the warmer months.

"Thank you. You don't look so bad yourself," she said with a sly smile. "Let me grab by purse."

As they walked down the steps to his brother's truck - which he was finally able to drive thanks to her therapy skills - it felt like old times. Like those first dates they'd had as kids so many years ago.

Nash opened the door for her, as he'd always done. Chivalry was something he'd learned from so many of the men in their small mountain town. Always open doors, pay for dates and walk on the outside so that the woman never gets mud splashed on her from the road.

"So this is Billy's truck?" Emmy asked as they drove toward the downtown area.

"Yes. Can't you tell by the mess in here?"

Emmy laughed. Billy had always been a mess. "What's that smell?"

"I think it's the old burger I found under the seat this morning. Sorry about that," Nash said, embarrassed. "I tried to cover it."

"With... what is that smell... cinnamon?"

"Actually, it's called Autumn Harvest," he said, holding up

an air freshener he'd stashed under the front seat. Emmy giggled. "Sorry. It was all I could find in the house."

"Maybe you need your own car."

"I have a vehicle back in Vegas," Nash said, not making eye contact.

"Of course."

They drove in silence for the rest of the way. Nash was always uncomfortable when the conversation turned toward Vegas. Emmy seemed tense when they talked about him going back there, and in reality, he was starting to feel weird about it too. The longer he was gone, the less it felt like home.

"Here we are," Nash said as they pulled up at his father's house. Emmy didn't move and looked straight ahead, her body stiff as a board. "You okay?"

"Yeah. I guess I just never thought I'd be here again." She looked at the house like she was staring through it.

"If you don't want to go in, I'll totally understand…"

"No. It's fine," she said after taking a deep breath. "I'm an adult now, and there's nothing he can say that will change my life like it did back then."

Nash felt guilty for not reigning his Dad in all those years ago, but what could he have done really? He was just a kid, and Brick was way more powerful than he was.

"Ready?" he asked as he came around and opened her door. Emmy reached down and took his hand as he helped her out of the truck. Billy sure did like his trucks to be high up in the air.

As they walked up the stairs, Nash had to wonder if this whole thing was a good idea or not. But it was too late. Emmy was about to come face to face with his father.

~

THE BUTTERFLIES in Emmy's stomach were apparently having a kickboxing match. Why was she so nervous? She wasn't dating Nash. She never had to see Brick again after this, and he had literally no power over her life as an adult.

And yet she felt her insides shaking like one of those cheap 70s motel vibrating beds her mother had told her about way too many times.

"Emmy!" Billy said, raising his beer bottle in the air from the kitchen. He looked the same as always with his big cowboy hat and scruffy beard that didn't fully grow in.

"Hey there, Billy," she said with a smile as he moved across the room and pulled her into a big hug.

"Don't smother her, man," Nash said, shooing his brother away from her after a few moments. Emmy quickly surveyed the room, but didn't see Brick or his fiancee.

"Come get something to drink," Billy said, pointing toward the kitchen area. Emmy followed him with Nash right on her heels, as if he was protecting her from some wild animal that might attack at any moment.

"So who else is coming?" Emmy asked.

"Well, Dad and Lana are upstairs getting ready. My new girlfriend, Anna, is coming…"

"New girlfriend?" Nash asked, a stunned look on his face. "When did this happen?"

"Oh, about three weeks ago now."

"Another one from the bar?" Billy wasn't known for having a longterm girlfriend. He was more of a "love 'em and leave 'em" kind of guy.

"No. Actually, I met her at one of the events. She runs a flower shop over off Elm."

"Is it serious?" Emmy asked.

Billy cleared his throat. "I think it might be."

"Wow! Someone is finally roping the elusive Billy Collier?"

"Well, I haven't brought up the idea of rope or typing each other up yet…"

"Gross," Emmy said, punching his arm playfully.

"But yeah, I think she could definitely convince me to shut down this whole dating operation and get one of those white picket fences."

Nash glanced at Emmy, his mouth hanging open a bit.

"Well, I can't wait to meet her then," Emmy said, smiling up at Billy.

They continued chatting beside the breakfast bar for the next few minutes until Emmy started hearing noises and realized it was footsteps coming down the stairs.

"You must be Emmy," a woman said, her voice peppy and welcoming. Emmy looked over to see the woman, who she assumed was Lana, standing there. She was beautiful and had one of the biggest smiles Emmy had ever seen. Before she could respond, Lana pulled her into a big hug like they'd known each other for years.

"Nice to meet you," Emmy said as they broke apart. "You must be Lana?"

"Yes, honey. I'm so sorry I didn't properly introduce myself before grabbing you for a hug!" She laughed loudly as Emmy glanced at Nash. He was smiling. He was comfortable here, and that made her happy.

"Lana, can you help me?" Billy called from the kitchen where it sounded like pots and pans were falling from the sky.

"Coming, honey!" she called as she trotted away.

"Hi, Emmy," Brick said from the bottom of the stairway. Emmy froze for a moment, feeling like she'd been pulled all the way back to being a scared teenager standing in front of this towering man.

"Mr. Collier," she said, her voice even and unchanging.

Nash swallowed so hard that Emmy could hear it. He was nervous too, apparently.

"Please, call me Brick. You're an adult now too," he said with something resembling a smile on his face. He seemed less frightening now. Maybe it was because she was an adult. Maybe it was because he was older and turning gray.

"Okay," Emmy said. "Thanks for letting me come to the cookout."

The conversation was stiff to say the least. Emmy kind of wanted to run straight out the front door and go back to her cozy cabin by the river.

"Hey, baby!" Billy suddenly yelled across the room. A young woman walked in with red hair and the biggest pair of blue eyes Emmy had ever seen. This must be Anna, she thought.

"Emmy and Nash, this is Anna," Billy said proudly. Emmy had never seen him smile so big.

"Nice to meet you, Anna," Emmy said, shaking her tiny, petite hand. If she had looked up the word "adorable" in the dictionary, Anna's face surely would've been there.

"Nice to meet you," she said back as Nash shook her hand too.

After all the pleasantries were exchanged, it was time to eat. Emmy made sure to stick close to Nash. The last thing she wanted to do was get stuck sitting next to Brick.

Surprisingly, dinner was easier than she thought it would be. Stories were shared, laughs were frequent. Emmy found herself enjoying the company of everyone, although she refused to make eye contact with Brick.

Even so, he seemed different. Nash was right. This woman had changed him. He looked at her with adoration on a frequent basis. He laughed and told jokes. He and Nash ribbed each other. It was like a real family, and nothing like the way Nash had been raised.

Emmy found herself thinking about how maybe people could actually change. After all, Steve had certainly changed, only in a bad way. And if people could change for the worse, couldn't they also change for the better?

"So, what'd you think?" Nash asked, walking up behind Emmy on the deck. She was enjoying the homemade vanilla ice cream that Lana had churned the old fashioned way while everyone else was inside playing a spirited board game of some kind.

"I had fun, actually," Emmy said quickly. Watching Nash smile gave her more butterflies.

He moved closer and leaned into her ear, his warm breath causing chills down her body. "Not as bad as you thought?"

Emmy turned to face him, realizing too late that his face was going to be so close to hers. "Not bad at all," she said. They both froze for a moment, only an inch or so between them, before being interrupted by Billy yelling out the door.

"Ya'll gonna play the next game or what?"

"I think we're going to skip it," Emmy said back. Billy grunted and shut the door as Nash stepped back a bit.

"You're trying to avoid my father, aren't you?"

Emmy bit her lips together. "Maybe."

"Em, I thought you were here for closure?"

"No... You said you needed closure, Nash. I'm here so you can get that with your father. But I don't need anything from Brick Collier."

The sound of Brick clearing his throat behind them caused Emmy to jump. There was no question he'd heard what she said.

"Sorry to interrupt. Just thought ya'll might want to join us for coffee." Brick closed the door without waiting for a response, and for some reason Emmy felt a little guilty. He really did seem different, but did that mean she had to forgive him?

~

"WELL, I'M STUFFED," Billy said, leaning back against the sofa and rubbing his stomach. Although he was tall and still as lean as their teenage years, he looked like he had a small baby bump after chowing down all day.

Brick was quiet and hadn't looked her way since hearing what she'd said on the deck earlier.

"Hey, Billy, I have to go," Anna said as she came back from taking a phone call on her cell.

"Really? Something wrong?"

"Apparently the alarm is going off at my shop, so I have to meet the alarm guys over there. We've been having problems with it."

"Dang. I don't want to miss seeing the fireworks with you. Why don't I come along and we can just meet everyone on the square a little later?"

Anna nodded, smiled and jetted out the door with Billy hot on her heels. It was just starting to get dark outside, so fireworks would be in a couple of hours. And truthfully, Emmy couldn't wait to get back to some semblance of normal. Being around Brick was making her stomach knot up so much that a Boy Scout couldn't get the thing untangled.

"Say, Nash, do you think you could help me with something upstairs?" Lana said suddenly. Emmy felt like she was going to throw up when she realized that would leave her sitting alone with Brick.

"Now?" Nash said, cutting a glance at Emmy, knowing full well she wasn't going to be okay with it.

"If you don't mind. Your Daddy's birthday is coming up, and I want to run something past you," she whispered with a sly smile.

Brick looked at Nash and threw his hands up. "What the lady wants, the lady gets. Just humor her."

Nash stood and squeezed Emmy's shoulder as he followed Lana up the stairs, glancing back one more time at Emmy.

Brick cleared his throat and leaned forward as if he was going to say something, but Emmy shot up from her chair and moved toward the kitchen.

"Jeez, where are my manners? The least I can do is help Lana clean up a bit in here…"

She could feel Brick following her to the kitchen. She grabbed a dish towel and started wiping down the non-wet counters.

"Emmy, I wanted to say…"

"Where are your anti-bacterial wipes? Salmonella is a dangerous thing…"

"We didn't eat chicken."

"Still, one can't be too careful." She was giggling nervously and was completely unable to stop which made her sound like a lunatic.

"Emmy." Brick only had to say her name in that way of his to get her attention. She stopped in her tracks, just like she was a kid again.

"Yes?" Finally, she looked up and made eye contact with him. He still made her a nervous wreck.

"While they're upstairs, I just wanted to clear something up."

"Not necessary, Mr. Collier. Really."

"Please call me Brick."

"I'd really rather not."

Brick nodded and sighed as he leaned against the counter. "I was a complete and total jackass back then, Emmy."

She chuckled under her breath. "Well, you're certainly right about that."

Brick smiled. "I'm very sorry for how I treated you. I know that doesn't make up for anything, but I want you to know that I'm not proud of how I acted or even who I was back then."

"Do you have any idea of how you hurt me? And Nash? We could've been together all these years."

"You still love Nash, don't you?"

Emmy swallowed hard. "My personal life isn't any of your business."

Brick walked to the refrigerator and took out a water. He opened it and took a long drink. "You're totally right. None of my business. But second chances are hard to come by in this life, Emmy. If you get that chance, don't waste it. Just a little piece of advice."

"I didn't ask for any advice," she said, staring down at the counter. She could feel her jaw clenching so hard that she'd probably need a dental visit after this conversation.

"I know you probably don't forgive me, Emmy. And that's okay. But please know that if my son loves you, which I think he does, and you don't want to be around me I'll understand. I'll do whatever I can to make you feel comfortable."

"You know what? I don't need you to make me feel anything. I'm fine!"

"Emmy, what can I do to make things right between us?" he asked, running his fingers through his still thick hair, much like Nash did when he got frustrated.

"She was your granddaughter," Emmy heard herself saying barely above a whisper.

Brick swallowed so hard that Emmy actually heard it. She looked over to see his eyes watering a bit, although he cleared his throat and turned the other direction when he saw her looking.

"It was a girl?"

Emmy took in a deep breath. "Yes."

"Does Nash know that?"

"I told him recently."

"My granddaughter," he said, barely above a whisper. After he gathered himself, he turned back toward her. She wasn't as nervous anymore. "I can't change the past, Emmy. I sure wish I could. There's a lot I would change. The crazy thing about age is that it allows you the benefit of looking back over everything in your life, but it's also like a prison because you can see it but you can't do a damn thing about it."

"I get that," Emmy said, thinking back to her own past and the things she would change if she could.

"I don't expect anything from you, but please don't punish my son for my misdeeds. He turned out to be an amazing man, despite the parents he had, thank God."

Emmy started to feel a softness in her heart. She didn't want to, and she definitely wasn't anywhere near ready to forgive Brick. But a part of her believed him, that he had regrets and had changed over the years.

"Look, I appreciate your apology. I really do. But right now, I can't promise anything will change as far as how I feel."

"I understand."

"Plus, Nash is leaving to go home to Vegas soon, so you and I don't have to see each other anyway."

"Everything okay in here?" Nash asked as he entered the kitchen, a worried look on his face.

"Yeah, everything's fine," Brick said, forcing a smile. Lana slid her arms around his waist and put her head against his chest.

"You about ready for some fireworks?" she asked, looking up at him adoringly. Brick smiled down at her. Emmy was so conflicted as she watched them. Who was this man?

"Nash, do you mind running me back by my house? I think I forgot my wallet."

"Sure. No problem. We'll see you guys later on," Nash said, giving Lana a quick hug and shaking his father's hand.

"Thanks for inviting me," Emmy said, ready to make her escape. Lana pulled her into a tight hug.

"Anytime, sweetie."

"Mr. Collier," she said, nodding her head at him.

"Emmy."

CHAPTER 13

*a*s they drove down the long road toward her house, Emmy was quiet. She just couldn't get her conversation with Brick out of her mind. And then when she'd said Nash was going home soon, his face had changed, almost like he was surprised to hear that. Had he not thought Nash would leave one day?

"You sure are quiet over there," Nash finally said, looking at her. "Did my Dad say something to upset you?"

Emmy smiled. "No. He actually apologized... more than once."

"He did? I bet that was a shock. Only a few people on Earth have heard Brick Collier apologize."

Emmy chuckled. "Yeah, it was a little jarring."

"So how did you feel about his apology?"

"I don't know yet. Still processing it, I guess. My mind definitely doesn't want to accept it, but my heart is giving me problems."

Nash smiled. "Your heart has always given you problems, Emmy Moore. And that's because you have a big heart."

Butterflies bounced around her stomach, Sometimes she

129

hated the way Nash made her feel because she knew it was ending soon. Thinking of letting him go back to Vegas made her heart ache.

"Here we are," Nash said as they pulled up in front of her house. "Want me to wait here?"

"Why don't you come inside for a bit? The fireworks don't start for at least another hour, right?"

Nash checked his watch and nodded before following her inside.

"Oh, I like what you've done with the entryway. Nice Feng Shui," Nash said.

Emmy looked at him and laughed. "Feng Shui?"

"I read a magazine article at my dentist's office once."

Emmy giggled at that. Nash could always make her laugh. "And what was this article about exactly?"

"Feng Shui and romance."

"What?"

"Yep. Apparently, the way you decorate can help you get more romance in your life," Nash said, looking around. "For instance, you have two candlesticks together right here."

"Okay…"

"Well, that enhances your chances of romance."

"Ah, I see," Emmy said, walking up beside him. "What else can I do to increase my chance for romance?"

Nash cleared his throat, the same way he always had when he got nervous. "Well, there are a few ways but I'd say the best way to increase your chance for romance is to skip the fireworks and stay here with me tonight."

Emmy's heart started pounding against her chest so hard that she was afraid an ambulance would need to be called.

"What?"

Nash turned around and looked at her. "I can't do this anymore, Emmy."

"Do what?"

"This cat and mouse game."

"I don't know what you..."

"Do you still have feelings for me?"

"What does it matter, Nash? This will all be over soon, and I'll be left holding the bag again. I can't put myself through that."

Nash took both of her hands. "Let me ask you this. If I left tomorrow and went back to Vegas, would you be upset?"

"Of course I would, Nash. I love having you here. I can't deny that."

"And if I spent tonight holding you and kissing you, would that make my leaving any worse?"

She looked up at him, and all she could see was the boy she'd fallen in love with so many years ago. All she wanted to do was get wrapped up in his arms and forget anything bad had ever happened in her life. The miscarriage. Him leaving her. Her marriage to Steve.

Tonight, she just wanted to be with Nash.

"One night," Emmy said, all the while knowing that one night with Nash was going to lead to a lifetime of wanting him.

HOURS HAD PASSED. Nash had texted his father, letting him know Emmy wasn't feeling well and they were just going to hang out at her house for the evening.

But this had been the best night of his life. Kissing her had taken him back to being a kid, but she definitely kissed like a woman these days.

They had slow danced to old songs, reminisced about old memories and held each other close all night. Tonight, they would make new memories that would last them a lifetime, but Nash was having a hard time picturing a lifetime without her.

As he laid back against the cushy sofa, her head resting against his chest, he tried to imagine a life without her. He tried to envision coming home for a visit and seeing her with someone else. Dating other men. Possibly marrying one. How would he feel about that?

He thought about his options, the ones she knew nothing about. The changes he was thinking of making in his life. The new man he wanted to become for her. For him.

He could feel her softly sleeping on his chest, and all he wanted was to feel that way every day of his life. But would he resent her for taking him away from his career? Was she taking him away? Or did a bull stepping on him already do that?

So many questions and feelings. And yet he felt more at peace right now than he had in years. Suddenly Vegas didn't feel like home. Whiskey Ridge didn't feel like home.

Emmy felt like home.

$\sim$

"GOOD MORNING, SLEEPYHEAD," Nash said as Emmy lifted her head from his chest. She couldn't recall ever sleeping so soundly in her life.

"Wow, how long did I sleep?" she asked, rubbing her eyes as she sat up. They were still piled on her sofa, sunlight peeking through the miniblinds.

"Let's see… about ten hours?" Nash said, smiling.

"Sorry. I guess I wasn't very good company. But I slept so well."

Nash stood up and pulled her into a hug. "I'm not complaining, Em."

"Oh, gosh, what time is it?"

"It's eight-fifteen..."

"I'm late for work!" she said, rushing around the living room like a bat out of hell.

"Em, it's okay! I called your assistant, and she said your first appointment cancelled this morning. You don't have anyone until eleven."

Emmy stopped running around and took in a deep breath. "Oh, thank God!"

Nash walked over to her and slid his arms around her waist from behind, pressing his lips to her ear. "I like taking care of you, Emmy Moore. You know that, right?"

Emmy smiled. She'd longed to hear that from him for so many years. But he was leaving soon, and she was falling fast. This wasn't good.

"Thank you," she said softly. One night. That's all it had been. One amazing night, and now it was over. They'd gotten the closure they needed. They'd missed the fireworks on the square in order to make fireworks of their own.

"Breakfast?" Nash asked.

"I'm starving."

"I think I saw you have some eggs in there. Why don't I whip up some French toast while you take a quick shower?"

"I could get used to this," Emmy said. Nash turned her around to face him.

"Last night was..."

"Amazing," she said, finishing his sentence. "I'll never forget it."

"Neither will I," he said, kissing her softly.

Emmy stepped back reluctantly. "Better go get ready so we have time to eat."

NASH STOOD on the deck at his father's house, staring out into the wooded expanse. When he'd first come back to Whiskey Ridge, it didn't feel like home anymore. Everything seemed foreign, and he'd wanted to board the first plane back to Vegas.

And then he saw Emmy.

Things were different, and that thought terrified him. What if he could finally have everything he ever wanted?

"Looking good, my boy," Brick said as he walked out on the deck. "Steady as I've ever seen you."

"Yeah. I'm feeling back to normal. Emmy's a miracle worker."

Brick leaned against the deck and looked out into the woods. "That she is."

"I think my therapy is almost over."

"You sound a little sad about that."

Nash cleared his throat. "Nah. I need to get back to regular life."

Brick laughed. "You don't really think I believe that do you?"

"Believe what?" Nash asked, turning toward his father.

"That you can leave her again."

"I don't have much of a choice, now do I? My career is in Vegas, and if I don't go back, I lose it all. My income, my reputation, my future."

"Is that what you see for your future, Nash? Riding bulls out West while Emmy lives right here in your hometown?"

Nash sighed and ran his fingers through his hair. "My choices are very limited, Dad."

"No, they're not. I want to talk to you about something…"

EMMY WIPED down her kitchen counters and looked out the window toward the river. She could just see the edge of the rock that Billy had jumped off of as a kid. Every time she saw it, it made her laugh.

Those really had been good times. And now Nash was going to be leaving her all over again.

The doorbell rang, so she tossed the dirty rag through the laundry room door as she made her way to the foyer.

"Nash? What're you doing here?"

Nash was standing there smiling. "I brought you a gift."

"A gift?"

He reached down behind the rocking chair that was beside him and pulled out the most gorgeous red wooden birdhouse. It was huge!

"Oh my goodness! How beautiful."

"I saw it in that bird feed store down on the square and thought you might like it. You can hang it on the deck and watch the birds through the window."

Emmy smiled. "Thank you. It's just wonderful, Nash. And I can think of you when I look at it."

Nash put the birdhouse down and put his arms around her waist, pulling her toward him. He kissed the top of her head.

"I need to talk to you."

"Okay, but first can you help me with something?"

"Sure."

"The dishwasher isn't working, and it leaked all over the floor this morning. Think you can take a look at it?"

Nash followed her inside. Sure enough, the dishwasher was leaking onto the hardwood floors, a trickle rolling down the stainless steel right onto the floor.

"I would call my landlord, but you know he's elderly and they're traveling…"

Nash crouched on the floor and started tinkering with it while Emmy put on a pot of coffee. Even though it was hot outside, she had to have her coffee. It was like the blood in her veins.

"That should do it," Nash said as he dusted off the front of his jeans.

"Mr. Fix It," Emmy said with a smile as she handed him a cup of black coffee. Nash's phone rang in his pocket.

He looked at the screen. "Dang. I need to take this. I'll be right back." He stepped out onto the front porch.

Emmy stood in the kitchen for a moment, watching him out the front window. He was so gorgeous. How was it possible he'd gotten more handsome over all these years?

Still, his face looked worried right now, like he was having an intense conversation with someone. She wondered who it was. Why were his eyebrows knitted together so tightly as he spoke?

Emmy couldn't help herself as she got closer to the window, which happened to be slightly cracked from her morning cleaning routine. Would it be so bad if she just listened in? Maybe she could help him with whatever the problem was...

"I don't know how I'm going to tell her, honestly. I hope she'll be happy for me, but I'm not sure..."

Tell who? Her? What did he need to tell her? Now she was more convinced than ever that she should listen in.

"You're right. I have to get back to my career before I don't have one. But I don't know how Emmy's going to feel about this..."

It was her. What was he keeping from her?

"I know it's time. I'm basically healed. I've stayed in therapy longer because I wanted to spend more time with her..."

Aw. That was nice.

"But the rodeo business waits for no one, ya know? I can't let all my years of hard work go to waste, and it's the only thing I'm trained to do anyway. So, yeah, I'll fly out to Vegas and…"

Emmy backed away from the window and leaned against the foyer wall. He was leaving soon. None of this had really meant anything to him. The moment she'd let her heart open for Nash Collier had been the moment she'd lost control of her life for the second time. She wasn't going to get knocked down in his wake yet again.

She quickly ran back to the kitchen and threw some cold water on her face. She wasn't going to cry. No way. She'd shed way too many tears over men in her life, and she wasn't doing it again.

"Sorry about that," he said as he walked back into the kitchen. "It was my Dad."

"Right. Okay. Well, listen, I've got a ton to do today, Nash. Thanks for fixing my dishwasher."

Nash looked confused. "Wait. Are you telling me to leave?"

"Kind of. No offense, but I have to go see my Mom and then I have some grocery shopping to do. Can we chat tomorrow at therapy?"

"Um… I guess so. It's just I had something I wanted to talk to you about…"

Emmy pushed on his shoulder, moving him toward the front door. "Okay then, so we'll talk more about that tomorrow. Be safe," she said, opening the front door. Nash stood there a moment and looked at her before he walked outside.

Emmy quickly shut the door and leaned against it before sliding down to the floor in a puddle of unwelcome tears.

CHAPTER 14

*N*ash was confused. He'd thought he was making strides with Emmy and that maybe they could be more than just friends. But the way she'd basically thrown him out of her house yesterday had confused him.

As he walked into therapy, he wondered if he'd made her angry in some way. Had he given her mixed signals? Had their night together been just that - one night?

"Good morning," he said when he saw her standing in the doorway of the therapy room.

"Morning, Nash," she said quickly. "Listen, we're going to get you started on the treadmill first today. Do twenty minutes on incline, and I'll check back with you after that."

Today, she was all business. No facial expression, very little eye contact. He just didn't understand it. It was like they didn't even know each other.

Was this her way of telling him they didn't have a future together?

The whole time he walked, he watched her. She didn't look his way. She worked with other patients, laughing and smiling, but apparently he didn't warrant that from her today.

When he finished, he got off the treadmill and stood beside it. Emmy walked over with papers in her hands.

"Congratulations, Nash. You've officially graduated from physical therapy. These are your release papers. I recommend you follow up with a qualified orthopedic doctor in Vegas, just to be sure you don't need to have a therapist on hand out there as well."

"Vegas? But I…"

She looked up at him, her face impassable. "I've got other patients, so I really can't talk much now. But, again, congratulations. I know you've been wanting to get back to your home, and I wish you the best."

And with that, she walked away.

EMMY DIDN'T WANT to go home. She knew Nash would likely be looking for her there, and she just couldn't deal with another goodbye.

He had a life in Vegas, and he needed - and wanted, apparently - to get back to it. As far as she was concerned, she'd done her job and done him a favor by helping him heal and then letting him go.

It was because she loved him that she was making it easy for him to leave.

"You want another glass of wine?" Debbie asked as they sat on her sun porch at the end of a long hard day.

"No thanks. No amount of wine is going to change how I feel."

"I'm sorry, Em. Honestly, I thought he'd stay."

"There's no reason for him to stay here, Deb. His career and life are in Vegas."

"Well maybe you could go there?"

"He didn't ask me, first of all. And I love my job here. Plus, my mother needs me whether she wants to admit it or not."

"Long distance relationships can sometimes work…"

"No."

"But do you really think freezing him out like this is the way to end things?"

Emmy sighed. "I hate doing this, Deb. But I have to protect myself this time, and I just can't do the whole emotional goodbye thing. It was devastating to lose Nash the first time. I can only imagine what a second time might do to me. This is self preservation."

"I wish I could help."

"Me too," Emmy said, leaning her head back against the chair.

～

NASH HAD CALLED multiple times and texted even more, but Emmy had ignored them. She'd taken a couple of days off work just to avoid seeing him if he stopped by. It was ridiculous really, but she just wanted a clean break.

She felt stupid for falling for him again, but that was exactly what she'd done. She'd promised herself that it was only a kiss… and then only one night… but things were never that way with Nash. They couldn't be.

She'd heard through the grapevine that he was leaving today. In fact, he was already on his way to the airport. It was over. He'd go back to his life, find a new love and that would be it.

She'd stay in Whiskey Ridge, grow old and gray and maybe take up knitting.

Okay, so maybe she was being a tad bit negative.

Days passed, and there were no more phone calls or texts. He'd gotten the message, apparently. While she should've been relieved, she wasn't. She felt empty.

~

"EARTH TO EMMY," Pauline said as she waved her hand in front of her daughter's face. Pauline had finally gotten around to going over to Emmy's new place for dinner.

"Sorry, Mom. I was just thinking about some stuff."

"You mean you were thinking about Nash," Pauline said pointedly before taking a drink of her sweet tea. Pauline had always been a sweet tea addict, often joking that the blood in her veins had been replaced with it years ago.

"Why do you say that?"

"Sweetie, it's the same lovesick look you had on your face as a teenager. I remember when Nash went out of town for the weekend and you sat around with that forlorn look on your face the whole dang time."

Emmy smiled. "Young love."

"Old love, young love. It's all the same. When you find the one for you, no one else will do. Hey, I'm a poet and didn't know it!" Pauline giggled at her own joke as Emmy thought about what she'd just said.

"He doesn't love me."

"I would beg to differ, Emmy. I've seen how he looks at you."

"He left me all over again."

"You sent him away this time, honey."

"What? No I didn't. I gave him what he wanted."

"Did you? Then why did he call and text and try to see you?"

"Maybe he wanted to say goodbye so he wouldn't feel guilty for leaving."

"Or maybe he wanted to stay, but he needed to know you wanted him to stay."

"You've read one too many romance novels, Mom."

"Maybe so. But you know what? The hero and the heroine of a good romance novel never give up on each other. They fight for their happy ending."

"Yeah, well sometimes there isn't a happy ending."

~

"WELL, Mrs. Banks, I do believe you're almost ready to get back to playing tennis," Emmy said to the older woman. She had to hand it to her; she was feisty and in good shape for a woman of her age.

"Good because I'm ready to take the title back from Estelle Goldman."

"Title?"

"The retirement village tennis tournament is coming up in six weeks. I need to get my trophy back."

Emmy smiled as she finished rubbing the woman's shoulder. "Well, I'll be rooting for you."

Emmy was glad it was the end of the day. She was tired and wanted nothing more than a pint of ice cream and a long hot bath. That was becoming her routine.

She missed him. No matter how many weeks it had been - three weeks and four days to be exact - Nash was never far from her mind. She'd even found herself looking online for news about the rodeo circuit out West. Nothing about him competing yet, but she did see where Deke had won a regional championship of some kind.

As she wiped down the therapy tables and locked up, she thought about the time she'd had with Nash. Those weeks of therapy. The dinner at his Dad's house. The night they'd spent together. It seemed like it all happened lightyears ago.

"Emmy?"

She turned to see Brick standing in the waiting area, his cowboy hat in his hand.

"Mr. Collier? What're you doing here?"

"I said you can call me Brick."

"And I said I don't want to."

Brick chuckled under his breath. "Fair enough."

"Why are you here?"

"We need to talk."

"Is Nash okay?" she asked, immediately worried that he'd been hurt, or worse.

Brick smiled. "He's fine. Well, physically he's fine."

Emmy walked closer. "Then I'm not sure what we'd need to discuss."

"He's lost without you, Emmy."

Her stomach tightened. "I doubt that."

"Well, you can doubt it all you want, but it's true."

"He left. I didn't."

"Didn't you?"

Emmy was getting irritated. "Can you stop speaking in riddles and just get to your point? I have ice cream waiting at home."

"You wouldn't answer his calls or texts. What was he supposed to do?"

"Nothing. I helped him heal and got him back to a life he loves. I wasn't going to beg him to stay even though..." Emmy stopped before she said too much.

"Even though you wanted him to stay?"

"Doesn't matter," she said as she walked behind him and flipped the sign to "closed".

"He didn't leave, Emmy."

"What?"

"He was never leaving you."

Emmy turned, confusion apparent on her face. "He's

in Vegas."

"No, he's not, actually."

"What?"

"He'd kill me if he knew I was talking to you, but I can't stand to see him like this anymore."

"Where is he?"

"Right now, he's in Tennessee. Coming home tonight."

"Tennessee?"

Brick leaned against the front counter. "I've never seen two seemingly smart people work so hard at not being together."

"Why was he in Tennessee?"

"Because Nash is running my company now. Lana and I are hitting the road in our motorhome so we can see the rest of this beautiful country. Nash was in Tennessee tying up some loose ends of a new circuit we're setting up there."

"Why didn't he tell me?"

"How could he? You shut him out. He thinks you don't love him, Emmy. That you just released him from treatment to get rid of him."

"But I heard him on the phone... he said he was ready to get back to it..."

"That was me. He was ready to get back to work."

"But he mentioned Vegas..."

"Yes. He had to go out there for a couple of days to meet with movers. His stuff was shipped here last week."

Emmy felt the blood drain from her face. How could she have been so stupid? And now Nash thought she didn't care.

"Oh my gosh."

Brick smiled and nodded. "Now you're getting it..."

"He probably hates me."

"He loves you, Emmy."

"Why did you tell me this? I think it's pretty safe to say you've never wanted me to be with Nash."

Brick sighed. "That's not true at all. I was a jerk back then, and all I could see was my dreams for my son. I never really thought about what he wanted, and the truth is that he has always wanted you. It wasn't until I met Lana that I finally realized what love was. Even old geezers can learn, Emmy."

She laughed. Maybe Brick wasn't so bad after all.

"What should I do?"

Brick smiled slyly. "I have an idea."

DRIVING BACK into Whiskey Ridge made Nash feel on edge. Being away for the last three weeks, between Vegas and Tennessee, had given him some distance. Some time to think. Time to consider what his life would be like living back in his hometown and running into the woman he would have to love from afar.

Why had she shut him out? It was a question that he'd pondered over and over again since the last time he'd seen her. Why had she practically pushed him back to Vegas?

"Damn it," he muttered to himself as he drove through town toward his Dad's house.

Thinking about Emmy was like one of those dang math problems he would stare at on his paper in high school. No matter how long and hard he thought about it, there was no answer that made any sense. And Nash liked answers. He liked concrete facts. And thinking about Emmy only created one big knot of emotions that he couldn't untangle no matter how hard he tried.

He wanted to have regrets about her, but he didn't. Every moment he'd ever spent with her was important to him. The only regret he had, besides leaving her all those years ago, was not meeting her earlier so he could've loved her longer.

"Damn it," he muttered to himself again. He was so frustrated with himself. Being lovesick was literally making him feel sick. He wanted to get hurt just so he could go back to therapy, just for a chance to see her and talk to her.

That was insane, he decided. Maybe he needed to see a local psychologist instead.

The sun was setting as he finally pulled up to his father's house. To his surprise, Brick's truck was gone, and Lana wasn't there either.

"Well, that's just great. Thanks for the welcome home, guys," he said to himself as he got out of the truck. "No homecooked meal for me tonight, I guess."

He grabbed his duffel bag from the bed of the truck and headed toward the front door. He unlocked the door and walked inside, immediately noticing how dark it was. Normally Brick left a small lamp on beside the foyer, but even it was off. He found himself getting a little worried.

He took off his hat and tossed it over the bannister before walking into the living room. And that's when he saw all of the candles lighting up the room and the breakfast bar in the kitchen. Country love songs started playing in the background.

"Hello?" he said, worried that he'd somehow walked in a romantic interlude between his father and Lana. That thought made him shiver.

"Hi, Nash," Emmy said as she walked out of the shadows.

"Emmy?"

Nash's stomach was really in knots now. Just seeing her face, even more radiant by the candlelight, made him want to scoop her up in his arms and never let her go.

But he was confused. Very, very confused.

HE WAS JUST STANDING THERE STARING at her, not moving a

muscle. Not running to her. Not taking her in his arms. Emmy was worried she'd gone too far setting up this romantic scene. Maybe his feelings had changed. Maybe Brick had played her for a fool.

"Emmy, what are you doing here?" he finally asked, still not moving toward her. He looked confused. Or maybe angry?

"I've missed you," was all she could manage to say. All of those words that she'd practiced on the drive over with Brick had flown right out of her head. Sure, she was poetic as heck when it didn't matter, but right now she could barely string two words together.

Nash laughed, but it was an ironic laugh with a little bit of frustration thrown in.

"You've missed me?"

"Of course I have,"

He sighed and leaned against the breakfast bar. "What are you doing to me, Emmy?"

"What?"

"You shut me out completely. I tried to reach you every way I knew how, and you just avoided me. And now you say you've missed me?"

"Nash, I didn't know…"

"Didn't know what?"

"That you were staying. That you were taking over for your Dad."

"I tried to tell you!"

She could tell how frustrated he was. "I overheard you on the phone that day at my house. I misunderstood and thought you were going back to Vegas."

"So you released me from treatment and then hid out until I left?"

Emmy took in a deep breath and nodded, looking down

at her feet. When he said it, it sounded like a middle school thing to do.

"I'm sorry, Nash. I should've answered your calls."

"Or my texts? Or answered your front door? Or gone to work maybe?"

"I really am sorry."

"And so you thought lighting a bunch of candles and playing some music was going to make it all better? Why are you even here in my Dad's house?"

"Brick came to see me. He told me everything and so I thought…"

"Yeah, well you thought wrong," he said before walking out onto the back deck and staring into the now darkened woods.

Emmy stood in the living room feeling like she was naked in front of the world. This had been a vulnerable thing for her to do, and now she just felt stupid. She grabbed her purse from the chair and walked out the front door.

~

NASH HEARD THE DOOR SLAM, and his heart sank. What had he just done? Emmy had lit candles, played music, apologized. And what had he done? Yelled at her and stormed out.

He knew what he wanted. He knew who he wanted. And yet he'd just done everything in his power to push all of that away… for the second time in his life.

Nash turned toward the house, intent on running out the front door and chasing her car down the street if he had to. But instead, he came face to face with an angry Emmy who had just stormed back into the house and out onto the deck.

"Emmy, I was…"

"No! You know what, buddy? You're going to listen to me right now," she said, pointing her index finger in his face.

"Okay…"

"I made a mistake pushing you away, but you don't get to be mad at me because it's nowhere near the mistake you made all those years ago and I was able to forgive you!" He wondered if she was going to take a breath at some point, but it didn't look like she would in the near future.

"Emmy…"

"Shut it," she said, holding up her hand. "I released you from treatment because I wanted what was best for you. I wanted you to live whatever life you wanted, and if that meant giving you up and living without you for a second time, I was prepared to do it. But don't you even think for one second that it didn't rip my heart out, Nash Collier. Don't think that I haven't cried every single day since then. But I loved you enough to let you go, if that's what you wanted!"

"It's not what I wanted, Emmy!" Nash finally interjected. "Can you just listen to me for a minute?"

Emmy sucked in a ragged breath and nodded, her hands firmly placed on her hips.

"Ever since the moment I saw you in the ice cream shop, I've known that I'd never go back to Vegas. There was no way in this world that I was leaving you for a second time."

"Then why didn't you tell me?"

"Because I didn't figure it out myself until we went to the river that day. I realized that if I never rode a bull again, I could live with that but there was no way I could live with not seeing you everyday for the rest of my life. But I didn't know if you still loved me, Emmy. I never thought you'd want to be with me again. I'm the guy who broke your heart and abandoned you when you needed me most, remember?"

"We've worked that out, Nash."

"You forgave me, Emmy. But that doesn't mean that I forgive myself."

Emmy's eyes welled up with tears as she stepped forward and took his hands. "This is our second chance, Nash. You're not getting rid of me this easily."

Nash smiled. "I never want to get rid of you, Emmy Moore."

She slid her arms around his waist and pressed her cheek to his chest. "Still mad at me?"

Nash pulled back and tilted her chin up. "Let's make a deal. From now on, shutting me out is never an option. Okay?"

"Okay. And leaving is never an option?"

"Agreed."

Emmy hugged him tightly and Nash knew that he had everything he would ever need.

EPILOGUE

The current was swift today, and the air was crisp. December in Whiskey Ridge could be unpredictable from year to year. Thankfully, it felt more like a cool Fall day than Christmas time.

In a few days, kids from all over town would be waiting up for Santa, but Emmy wasn't thinking about that. Instead, she was looking around at all of the most important people in her life. Her mother, Debbie, Deke, Lana, Billy, Nash, and yes, even Brick.

She stood there in her white gown, feeling the breeze blow her hair. The deck of her little rental house was one of her favorite places on Earth, which is why she and her new husband would be living there instead of Brick's large house.

"I can't believe you're my wife," Nash whispered in her ear as he slid his arms around her from behind. They looked down at the rock where they'd taken their vows just an hour ago. It had been everything Emmy had ever imagined.

"And I can't believe you're my husband," she said as she sank further into his embrace.

"Hey, don't be starting to honeymoon until we all leave, okay?" Billy joked as he walked up behind them.

"I can't promise anything," Nash said with a laugh. "I mean look at her in this dress."

Emmy pulled back and twirled around as she laughed.

"I think the point of the honeymoon is to keep her out of any dress, brother," Billy said.

"Billy, quit being vulgar!" Anna said as she walked up and slapped him on the arm. Billy chuckled before lifting her off the ground and planting a kiss on her forehead. Emmy had never seen him happier and expected a wedding announcement from Billy in the immediate future.

After all, weddings were becoming a regular thing in the Collier family. Brick and Lana had gotten married in November in the pavilion at the square, and they were about to hit the road again.

Billy and Anna were living at Brick's house, mainly to take care of it but Emmy was much happier in her little home by the river. It just fit her and Nash. Their happiest memories were just outside of their window.

"Congratulations again, you two," Lana said as she joined everyone on the deck. "You looked beautiful, my dear." She pulled Emmy into a hug, as she always did.

"My baby was a beautiful bride, wasn't she?" Pauline said. She and Lana had become fast friends lately. Lana had lunch with Pauline anytime she and Brick were back in town.

"Thank you, Momma."

"Hey, where'd everybody go?" Brick asked as he walked outside. He and Emmy had slowly worked on forging a new relationship and leaving the old behind.

It occurred to Emmy that this was the perfect wedding for her. Small, cozy, intimate. And all the most important people in her favorite place on Earth.

"Hey, Emmy, can I talk to you for a minute?" Brick asked.

Nash looked at his father as if he was questioning what was going on. "It's okay, son. I promise."

"It's fine," Emmy said, shooting a smile at her new husband. "He is my father-in-law, after all."

Everyone walked back inside, leaving Emmy alone with Brick as the sun started to set over the water.

"First, I want to tell you how happy I am that you and Nash finally ended up together, Emmy. He adores you, and we're so happy to have you as a real part of our family now."

"Thank you. I really appreciate you saying that."

"And I hope you'll take this in the spirit in which it's being given." Brick pulled an envelope out of his jacket pocket and handed it to Emmy.

She slowly opened it and pulled out a piece of legal paperwork. "I don't understand. What is this?"

"Well, that's the deed to this home."

"What?"

"I hope I didn't overstep, but I know how you and Nash love this place. So I bought it, plus the acreage around it in case you want to expand one day. Of course, I put it in your name, Emmy."

Emmy stared at him for a moment. "Why did you do this, Brick?"

"Because we're family, and believe it or not, I love you like my own daughter, Emmy. And if you want to live here, I don't want there to ever be a chance you'd lose this place."

"I don't know what to say. Thank you…"

"There's one more thing."

"There's more?"

"You won't be hearing from your attorney or any collection agencies in regard to your ex-husband anymore."

"What?"

"I might be an old country boy at heart, but I know how to negotiate. I know how to lean on people. And I wanted you to have a fresh start, Emmy. I hope you don't mind that I may have interfered just a tad."

"Brick, this is too much," she said.

"Emmy, we have history, and it wasn't always good. Just take this as my way of trying to make up for what I said and did back then."

Emmy instinctively hugged him. "Thank you so much, Brick."

"Everything okay out here?" Nash asked as he walked up.

"Everything is perfect," Emmy said, beaming as she looked up at him. And everything was perfect.

"I'll leave you to it. Congratulations, son. You've got a good one here," Brick said as he squeezed his son's shoulder and walked back inside.

"What was that all about?" Nash asked.

"Long story. I'll tell you all about it later."

"Later, huh?" Nash said as he pulled her close and pressed his lips softly against hers. "Got any plans for right now?"

Emmy peeked around his shoulder and looked through the sliding glass doors leading into the house. "Well, since the only person that seems to be left is your friend Deke, I'd say that our immediate plan should be to push him down the front stairs, lock the doors and get this honeymoon started."

"Ooooh, Mrs. Collier, I do like how you think!" Nash said, planting kisses down her neck. "Oh, Deke… can you meet me on the front porch?"

Emmy stood on the deck and watched Nash usher his friend out the front door. And as she turned and looked at the river below her, she imagined that one day her children would play in those same waters and maybe even jump from those same rocks, and she smiled.

≈

WANT to read more books by Rachel Hanna? Visit Amazon to find these other great titles!

THE JANUARY COVE SERIES:
The One For Me
Loving Tessa
Falling For You
Finding Love
All I Need
Secrets And Soulmates
Sweet Love
Choices of the Heart
Faith, Hope & Love
Spying On The Billionaire
Second Chance Christmas

THE WHISKEY RIDGE Series
Starting Over
Taking Chances
Home Again
Always A Bridesmaid
The Billionaire's Retreat